A Winning Hand Loses

I0542474

Alfie Robins

Kings Town Publishing

Kings Town Publishing, 2016.

British Library Cataloguing in Publication Data
A CIP catalogue record for this book is available from the British Library

ISBN: 978-09927594-6-9

About the Author

Alfie Robins was born and raised in the English east coast city of Kingston Upon Hull, known locally as, 'Ull. Alfie left school at 15 and started work as a ships carpenter working on the trawlers on Hull fish dock. Over the years he has had a varied career, carpenter, production manager in the caravan industry and sales manager with a radio communications company, to name but a few. He is now retired and concentrates on his writing. Alfie has three grown up children, two grandchildren and lives with his wife and son in rural East Yorkshire, England.

Also by Alfie Robins

Reprisal

Snakes and Losers

Why Won't You Stay Dead

Just Whistle

Funeral Rites

To be published in August 2016

Suits and Bullets

Acknowledgements

Once again, I would like to give special thanks to my family for their encouragement and constructive, but not always welcome criticism during the process of writing this book.

Thank you all.

The novel is based on the present day Hull and East Yorkshire. Also, Hull as it used to be during its heyday as the UK's premier fishing port. The majority of locations do exist in Hull and the surrounding area, on the other hand, others exist purely in my imagination.

For Harrison when he is old enough.

A Winning Hand Loses

Chapter 1

Detective Chief Inspector Philip Marlowe ran the palm of his hand across his grey stubble whiskers as he relaxed in his comfy office chair. The chair had seen better days, but he wasn't about to part with it any time soon. He pushed back and raised his legs, feet up on the desk, thinking maybe his shoes could do with a polish. His colleague, Detective Inspector Dave Gowan sat on the office two-seater sofa with his long legs stretched out before him.

'So, Phil, have you decided what you're going to do with your leave?' asked Gowan. It had been a hard few months for the team, one major incident after the other and they were due a rest. It had been a while since the DCI had the luxury of a decent break away from work, and this time nothing was going to stand in his way.

He hooked his arms behind his head and smiled. 'I've booked a small cottage in Whitby for two whole weeks, it's about time Archie and me had a bit of R and R away from this place.' Archie was Marlowe's four legged companion. He had been part of his divorce settlement and woe betides anyone who referred to him as "the dog". 'Soon as I've finished my coffee, I'm away to pack.'

'I'll leave you to it, then,' Gowan stood up un-scrambling his long frame from the low sprung sofa. At the same time adding a few more creases to his already well worn suit in the process. 'Have a good one, Phil,' he said as he opened the door to leave.

'Thanks, Dave, I will and, Dave, do NOT call me, not even if the station burns down!' Marlowe was adamant nothing was going to spoil their holiday.

Robert Arthur Bacuss, better known as Rab was at a loss. A black cloud of depression hung heavy over the twenty year old. What was going to happen to him? He had been to hell and back again. Was there no end in sight to his torment? He had plenty of time to think back to the day it all started - if only he hadn't been so greedy....

The smoke from Jamaica's finest "Virginia" spliff curled up to the ceiling of the small first floor apartment. The flat screen television on the wall tuned in to a music channel playing in the background. A two litre plastic bottle of extra strong cider lay on its side, its contents ready to spill onto the hardwood flooring. White Lightening cider was not his usual choice of drink, but he was going through a tight patch and money was short. Rab sat cross legged on the floor, barefoot. His jeans were carefully ripped at the knees and he was wearing a genuine retro 1960s "Mod's Rule" T-shirt.

He stretched out his right arm and grabbed the bottle around the neck, brought it to his lips and gulped down the coarse alcohol. He stood the bottle back on the floor, wiped his mouth with the back of his hand and looked at the cards he was holding in his free hand.

'Looks like I win again,' he said with a broad smile on his face as he threw the cards down. 'Mine I think - thank you very much.' He helped himself to the pile of plastic poker chips on the floor between them. 'Not very good at this are you, Mick?'

'Just having a run of bad luck, that's all.' Mick Harrison was just about the worst poker player there was. He only ever played for pennies. He had better things to do with his money, he needed it to live.

'How much is it you owe me now?' Rab asked as he picked up the cards and started shuffling the pack. 'Oh yeah, fifteen quid if I'm not mistaken.'

Mick stretched out his legs and stood up, brushing his fringe from over his eyes. 'Don't worry, you'll get your money,' he said sharply as he grabbed the cider bottle, unscrewed the cap and took a swallow before standing up and then dropping down on the sofa.

'Only winding you up, Mick, just playing for fun - right?' Rab stood up, walked over and sat next to Mick then poked him in the ribs with his elbow. 'Just joshing, pal.' He lay back on the cushions. 'Got a problem, mate, I need to make some cash - quick, any ideas?' He reached into his jeans pocket, took out his tobacco tin and skinned up.

'What's the trouble, won't daddy get his wallet out?' Rab and Mick had become friends during the Universities "fresher's" week, two years previous.

'You could say that. Me and the old man have had words. We had a barny about money, the greedy old git told

3

me it was about time I started to fend for myself - stopped my allowance. Tosser. Don't know how he thinks I'm going to manage.'

Mick and Rab got on well enough, but they were hardly bosom buddies. When it came to upbringing Rab and Mick were like chalk and cheese. Rab had been bought up in a totally different family environment to his friend, one where cash was not a shortage. All his life he had only to ask for something and it was there. He told people that his father was a carpet salesman, when in fact he was actually the owner of a very successful carpet retail store, *Excel Flooring UK Ltd*.

'It depends on how desperate you really are?'

'I'm more than desperate, mate, I'm well and truly skint,' he put the rollie to his lips, sparked up and blew a plume of smoke to the ceiling.

'I have some mates who have a regular poker school, pretty casual like, want me to see if I can get you in?'

If truth were known both young men used each other for convenience as the need arose. On this occasion Mick thought that maybe he could turn his mate's financial predicament to his own advantage. Perhaps he could make a few quid himself and teach Rab a lesson at the same time. He would introduce him to friends from his other life, people who would have no scruples when it came to separating Rab from his cash.

'Don't know, mate, I mean, they won't be playing for pennies will they?' Although he was pretty good, no, not pretty good, he thought he was exceptional when it came to poker. But at the same time he was really used to playing with his peers.

'Up to you, you said you were desperate, only trying to help.'

'Yeah, I know you are, mate.' He took another deep draw, held the smoke in his lungs and then blew it up to the ceiling.

'Give us that,' Mick reached out for the spliff. 'I can make a call if you want, have a think,' he passed back the spliff.

Rab sat quiet for a minute or two, wondering if he was actually good enough. He didn't know why he doubted himself, he *knew* he was a top poker player. Rab didn't waste too much time thinking. Any chance to get some cash was better than none.

'Go on then, it'll make a change playing for real money instead of piddling pennies, see if you can set it up,' he said confidently.

Bacuss had taken the bait, Mick knew he would. He was such a greedy bastard. Mick smiled to himself and stood up to leave. 'I'll text you later with the details.'

Rab nodded. 'Cheers, mate,' he mumbled as his drug fuddled eyes closed. He didn't hear Mick close the door as he left.

Once out in the street Mick took out his mobile and punched in a series of numbers.

'Mick, haven't heard from you in a while what can I do for you?' A voice at the other end asked.

'How do you fancy making us some serious money?'

'Always, Mick, always.'

'Then I think I know how...'

Mick Harrison wasn't like Rab, he didn't come from a privileged background. Mick came from a working class home in West Hull, and not a very good one at that. He had a drunken father who was handy with his fists and a mother who had to work three jobs to support his old man and his two sisters. Mick, he was the "black sheep" of the family - in reverse, in as much as he strove to get away from his roots by bettering himself. He had worked hard at school and gained a place at the University of Hull, but used his contacts from his dubious past life to support himself. In short, he was a bit of a "Jack the Lad".

An hour or so later Rab came out of his self imposed coma, stood, stretched and put his iPod into its dock. Vintage Pink Floyd bellowed around the room as he lay back on the sofa with the remains of the cider. Then came a hammering on the door.

'Yeah, yeah, I hear you,' he yelled as he stood up stumbled his way across the living room. 'Oh, it's you, thought you was going to text?' he said as he opened the front door.

'Changed my mind didn't I, thought I'd come in person to tell you it's all sorted,' Mick told him as he walked in. 'But you're gonna need some stake money.'

'How much?' Rab asked.

'A couple of hundred quid should do it.'

The reply was casual as if money was no object.

'That's me done then before we even get started. I've told you I'm skint.'

'Can't you tap up the old man or your step-mum? It's a chance to win some serious dosh.'

'No chance with the old man. Suppose I could try and get the money from Karen. Oh sod it, when is the game?'

'Friday night, in the back room of the *Blacksmiths Arms*.'

Rab had three days to get his stake.

Chapter 2

'Robert, I wasn't expecting to see you - come to see your dad?' asked Karen his stepmother, as he walked through the back door into the spacious designer kitchen. Karen wasn't the evil step-mother type, they actually got on quite well.

'It's not Dad I wanted to see, it's you. I was wondering if I could borrow some money?' He sat down at the breakfast bar, took the lid off the biscuit barrel and helped himself.

'Oh, Rab, you know what your dad's like, if he found out I've been lending you money... you know, the way you left things'

'Oh come on, Karen, he doesn't need to know. I won't tell him if you don't.' He gave her his best smile as he munched on his custard cream.

Karen shook her head and returned the smile. 'What are you like? I suppose so, how much do you need?' she asked reluctantly.

It always worked - the smile.

'£230 should cover it.'

'Oh! I wasn't quite expecting that!'

'I wouldn't ask if it wasn't important, you know that. It's for study material, £230 will cover everything I need until the end of the semester.' Rab lied through his teeth as he helped himself to a glass of juice.

'You'll get me in right bother one of these days.' Karen replied as she went into the lounge and came back with her purse in her hand. 'Don't mention it to your dad, we don't need any more arguments.'

Luckily for Rab his step-mother was a walkover.

'You're a star.' He leaned forward and kissed her on the cheek. 'I'll pay you back, promise.' After the obligatory small talk, he left the house with £230 in his wallet. The extra thirty pounds were to be spent wisely on take-a-ways and beer.

Come Friday, the day of the poker game, Rab was feeling lucky. Okay his stomach fluttered with a touch of nerves, but if he could win, he would be in a position to settle a couple of debts and tell his old man and his money to sod off. Early that evening Mick paid Bacuss a visit. Rab tried his best not to let the nerves show.

'Here you go, Mick,' he passed over a can of lager.

'Ta, you ready for tonight?' asked Mick as he accepted the can of cheap booze and dropped down onto the sofa.

'As ready as I'll ever be. These blokes, the fellas I'll be playing against, you known them long?'

'Since I was a kid, decent blokes. But not as good as you when it comes to poker.' Mick added trying to build up Rab's confidence. 'You'll take 'em to the cleaners.'

'That's good enough for me.' His voice lost its nervous edge. Mick was quick to pick up on the new found confidence.

'I tell you, Rab, it'll be like taking sweets from a kid,' he said trying to build up Rab's confidence further. 'You've

nothing to worry about, drink your lager then we'll be off.'
Rab did as he was told.

The *Blacksmiths Arms* was situated in a narrow cobbled
side street on Commerce Lane, between Hessle Road and
English Street, not exactly on the Hull tourist trail. The area
was Mick's old stomping ground, an area he knew like the
back of his hand. *Blackies* was once the local hostelry for
the nearby CD Holmes Ship Builders and brass foundry, in
what was once a thriving industrial area. The foundry like
the other heavy industrial businesses in the area had closed
their gates a long time ago, at the same time the *Blacksmiths
Arms* lost the majority if its clientele.

The boys caught a bus to the city centre and visited *The
Punch Hotel* for a pre-game drink, Rab was desperately in
need of some Dutch courage before the fifteen minute walk
to the *Blacksmiths Arms*.

'How are you feeling, ready to take 'em to the cleaners?'
Mick asked, doing some shadow boxing as they turned
down by the *Vauxhall Tavern* into St James Street.

'Absolutely, pal,' Rab answered confidently inside, he
was a bag of nerves. 'But give us a few minutes will you?' He
opened his tobacco tin and took out an already rolled spliff
and lit-up.

'You sure you're alright, mate?'

'Yeah will be in a minute, just a couple of drags to sort
my head.'

Heads turned as Mick and the young gambler walked
into the bar of *Blackies.* Not for the first time Rab began to
have doubts, wishing he was somewhere else.

10

'Two bottles of lager please, Suzie,' Mick asked as they crossed to the bar.

'Coming up, Mick, haven't seen you for a while how have you been keeping?' Suzie asked as she reached under the bar for the bottles.

'Don't get down this way very often these days. Been busy at Uni, you know how it is. This is my mate Rab,' he said, giving Bacuss a dig in the ribs. Rab smiled at Suzie.

'Here you are, lads,' pushing the bottles across the bar.

Mick stood at the bar resting on his elbows, next to him Rab resisted the urge to turn and look around the place. He sensed someone approaching them, but still remained focused on the optics behind the bar. In the mirror behind the optic rack he saw a man approaching, leather jacket, denim jeans and hair brushed back Elvis style, he looked well hard - scary.

'Alright, Mick?' The six foot something, leather jacketed biker asked as he slapped Mick on the back. 'This your mate, then?'

'Yeah, I'm not bad mate. This is Rab, Rab - Paul.'

'Paul Armstrong,' Paul held out his arm to shake hands. 'Good to meet you mate, Mick tells me you're a bit of a player?'

'Yeah, I can hold my own,' Rab blurted out cockily without thinking.

'I like confidence, see you in the back room in about half an hour, okay? Suzie, give the lad's another drink.'

'Looking forward to it. Cheers,' a tense Rab replied, picking up his bottle and knocking half of it back in one go.

Paul returned to his table.

'Steady up, mate, we don't want you half pissed before the game.' Both the young men laughed, one more than the other.

'He seems alright,' Rab replied, slightly apprehensively.

'Solid, Paul is. Looks tough, but he's a pussy cat, a top bloke.' Rab tried to hide the anxiety in his laugh.

'What's he do for a living?'

'Got a small scrap yard, runs it with the bloke over there, Eddie.'

Rab risked a quick glance. Like Paul, Eddie was dressed in biker type gear, jeans and studded denim jacket over a white T-shirt, he was heavy set with a round face that sported a full beard.

Mick saw the apprehension on Rab's face. 'Likes to look hard, goes with the image, but that's all it is - bullshit.' He tried to say it with conviction.

The back room of the *Blacksmiths* wasn't exactly a salubrious place, no bigger than the average living room with four battle scarred wooden tables and chairs, cigarette burned black and white lino covered the floor. Faded photographs of Hull trawlers and the old fish dock, covered the walls; literally, there was hardly an empty space on the nicotine stained walls.

Paul made the introduction. 'Lads, this is Rab,' he said with an arm around his shoulder. 'That scruffy looking fella is Eddie, he's my business partner.' Rab nodded to the bearded biker. Eddie reached across and gripped the younger man's hand firmly. Paul continued his introductions around the table. 'These two miserable gits are Tommy and George.' They all shook hands friendly. Rab thought maybe it would be okay after all.

'Good luck mate, see you in a bit.' Mick patted his pal on the shoulder and went back through to the bar.

'Right lads, introductions made, are we ready to play some poker?' Paul asked the three other men sat around the table. He didn't wait for a reply, ripped the cellophane of a new pack of cards and started to deal with the nimbleness of a professional player. Three hands in and Rab was sweating, he was the best part of a hundred fifty pounds down and was beginning to wish he'd never heard of Paul and the *Blacksmiths Arms*.

'We'll have to knock off for a bit, I need a piss,' said Eddie.

'Yeah, why not, let's grab a sandwich at the bar before we carry on,' replied Paul as the card school broke up leaving their cards and cash on the table. In the bar, a large plate of sausage sarnies was set out ready and waiting.

'How's it going?' Mick asked his mate as he came over and stood beside him, sliding over a pint - it was cheaper than a fancy bottle of imported piss.

'Not too good, Mick, only fifty quid left, then I'm skint - again.'

'You never know your luck could change. Grab a sarnie.'

'No thanks, I'm going outside for a fag.' Rab walked out the door and stood around the corner, took out his tobacco tin and skinned up. Standing outside the pub with his roll-up, he was in half a mind to do a runner, then thought better of it. Like the true gambler, he was, he believed his luck would change.

It did. Lady Luck was to smile on Rab that night, he won the next three hands, lost one and won a further four.

'That's me out,' Eddie said, throwing down his cards.

'You're not the only one,' said Paul, 'I'm skint, nowt left. Any objections if we call it a night?' he asked, looking around the table.

No objections.

Rab, was secretly pleased. He wanted out, his nerves were shattered, he just wanted to get out the place and have a smoke. He'd finished the night with eight hundred pounds in his back pocket.

'Not a bad night's work, lad,' Paul said as they walked out of the back room.

'Just luck,' replied Rab.

'Luck my arse. It was skill, I tell you, Rab, it's been a real pleasure playing with someone who knows a bit about cards. Give the lad a drink will you, Suzie?'

'Thanks.' Rab soaked it up, the compliment raised his mood, he felt on top of the world as he sipped from the bottle.

He loved praise, he always had.

'There's a game on Sunday night if you fancy it? We usually play twice a week, just friends like tonight, nothing too heavy.'

Rab gave it some thought - briefly. 'Thanks, I'll take you up on that.' Rab drank his bottle as quick as he could, he needed a smoke. 'I'm getting off now, Mick.'

'Hang on mate, stay and have another.'

'No thanks, Mick, feel as if I've had a skinful, see you tomorrow?'

'No probs, mate, I'll call around in the morning.'

'Till Sunday,' Paul said as he watched Rab leave.'

Rab left the pub, leaving Mick with his old friends. Eight hundred pounds, he couldn't believe it. Enough to pay his step-mother back, clear his debts, have a few quid in his pocket and still have a stake for the next game. He always knew his luck had to change sometime.

There was a lot of back slapping and laughter going on in the bar of the *Blacksmiths Arms* once Rab left the building. 'Nice one, Mick lad, where did you find him?' George, one the card players asked.

'I take a couple of classes with him at Uni. He's not a bad bloke, but he thinks he's the dog's bollocks when it comes to poker, always fleecing some poor sod and leaving them skint with nothing to live off.'

Although Mick did kind of like Rab, he didn't like the way he cajoled those who could ill afford to lose to join a game, and then laughed as he left them broke. Mick thought it was about time that Robert Arthur Bacuss felt what it was like to be on the receiving end. With the help of Paul and his old mates, Mick set up his own scam with the intention of fleecing him good and proper.

Chapter 3

Next morning, bright and early Marlowe loaded up the Mondeo with all he and Archie would need for two quiet weeks on the North Yorkshire coast. The roads were reasonably stress free, the main holiday season now over with, and approximately two hours later drove into Whitby.

With his companion Archie, a black and white, short legged, long eared dog of questionable parentage, he was determined to enjoy his autumn break. Marlowe had rented an eighteenth century stone built fisherman's cottage along Church Lane, at the foot of the famous 199 Steps that led down the hill from Whitby's ancient abbey. Though the cottage was small it had all Marlowe needed for a break away from routine - he was just pleased to be out of the city for a while.

Cosy, is how Karen, Marlowe's ex-wife would have described the cottage, then again, she *was* a bit of a snob. He was quite content with the small sitting room, a kitchen-diner, two bedrooms and a bathroom, it was perfect for Marlowe and Archie, even quite luxurious when you compared it to living on a narrow boat. *Fisherman's* cottage was the ideal hideaway for a couple of weeks rest and relaxation, away from the bustle of the city and pressure of the job.

Marlowe remembered Whitby fondly from his childhood, the beach, the harbour, the fish and chips. Most of all he remembered the Gothic Abbey that had served as his introduction to stories of the macabre, the inspiration behind Bram Stoker's classic tale, *Dracula*. He and his companion had every intention of enjoying the peace and quiet of North Yorkshire. Twenty four hours later, Marlowe was already on the way to establishing himself as a regular in the *Duke of York* public house, "*a procurer of real ale and fine home cooked foods*".

Saturday morning Rab woke early, still on a high from the previous nights win. He went through to the bathroom for a pee and was just washing his hands as the doorbell rang. Still in his boxers he answered the door. It was Mick armed with two takeaway cups of coffee.

'Bit early aren't you?'

'Been up a while. Good night, last night, eh?' He praised as he walked in.

'Brill mate, it was wicked. I came away with eight hundred smackers, fan-fucking-tastic.' He went through to the bedroom to put on a T-shirt and came back pulling up his jeans. 'Top night,' he said as he took his wallet from the back pocket of his jeans, opened it and took out a fifty pound note. 'For you, mate, thanks to you I'm back on track.'

'Na, it's ok, it's yours, you won it,' Mick protested mildly.

'Take it, you got me the gig, it couldn't have worked out better,' Rab insisted.

'Well, if you're sure, I could do with it, cheers.'

'If I have a night like that tomorrow, we'll both be laughing. It's about time the cards fell my way.'

If only you knew, come Sunday night you'll be laughing on the other fucking side of your face thought Mick.

The more Rab thought about it, the more he convinced himself he'd been playing with amateurs. Paul and his pals weren't in the same league, he was the tops. Later that night in the Universities Sanctuary Bar, Rab didn't hesitate in flashing the cash, buying drinks for all and sundry. Bragging to anyone who would listen to his tales of daring do with professional gamblers. Tales of how he'd pissed all over them and he was going to do the same again on Sunday night. Mick on the other hand, sat quietly and listened, knowing the truth he gave praise when he thought it appropriate.

Rab woke mid-morning Sunday with a banging headache. He cursed himself for drinking so much. Then again, he'd had a great night - even if he hadn't pulled and had come back to the apartment alone. He popped a couple of paracetamol with his coffee, he didn't intend to do much other than pay a flying visit to his step-mother to clear his debt. The rest of his day was spent doing nothing but chillaxing in front of the television watching re-runs of *Dave*. Rab had made arrangements to meet Mick in the *Punch Hotel* in Queen Victoria Square for a quick one, from there they would head to the *Blacksmiths*. He hoped it was a lucky routine. Feeling flush Rab phoned for a taxi – after all he could afford it.

Mick was already half way through his second pint by the time Bacuss arrived. 'How you doing mate?' He gestured for the barmaid to pull a pint for Rab.

'Sound as a pound, looking forward to it.' He was brimming with confidence. Mick could see it in his eyes.

'Haven't spent all the cash have you?' Mick asked seriously.

'You are jesting! Step-mum paid back, debts cleared, two hundred notes in my wallet ready and waiting to multiply.'

Arrogant pratt thought Mick. 'Well, we'd better drink up then and get to *Blackies* so you can double your money.' They both laughed and downed their drinks.

'You know this part of the city well?'

'Yeah, I was brought up here on Hessle Road. Mam and the girls live on Gypsyville now. My old man still lives around here, but I don't bother with him much. Only time he gets in touch is when he wants to tap me up for cash.' The rest of the journey was taken up with small talk about cards, girls and more cards, the latter of which held little interest for Mick. They paused as they reached the bar entrance of the *Blacksmiths Arms*. 'Ready, matey?'

Rab nodded. 'As I'll ever be,' he took a deep breath.

'Okay, let's go get 'em.'

The young men entered the bar with a flourish and smiles on their faces. 'Mick, Rab lad, glad you could make it,' Paul said as he walked the length of *Blacksmiths* bar to shake hands with the younger man.

'Here you are, fellas,' Paul slid two pints of lager down the bar, 'cheers.'

'Cheers, Paul,' they said in unison.

'Mick, you got a minute?'

Rab watched Mick follow him to the far end of the bar where an animated conversation took place. Mick didn't look too happy. "No way, I don't want sod all to do with it", Rab heard Mick say, as he turned his back on Paul and came to stand besides Rab.

'What was all that about?' asked Rab.

'Nowt, just Paul being a twat as usual. Not a bad pint this,' he said, picking up his pint and changing the subject. Mick was not happy, not happy at all. As the poker school went through to the back room, Mick walked out of the front door.

The game started well, two hands in and Rab was up two hundred pounds. Paul read the younger man's face like a book, he was brimming with confidence. The time was right, he gave a prearranged signal to Eddie.

'Fancy upping the stakes a little?' Suggested Eddie. 'Give me a chance to get some of my cash back?'

'It's a friendly game remember?' Paul replied convincingly.

'Oh come on you old miser,' cajoled Eddie. 'Jesus, it's not as if you're skint.' Rab looked from one to the other, this was just what he wanted, the chance of a bigger pot. A couple of wins and he'd take his leave and be away. 'What do you reckon, Rab?'

'I'm easy, it's ok with me if everyone else agrees.' He was praying they'd agree. He couldn't do anything but win.

'Ok, I'm not having you call me a tight arse.' Paul took more cash from his wallet and lay it on the table.

The cards were duly dealt. Rab won three further hands, he was £650 up and brimming with confidence. He was on a roll, nobody could touch him.

Then things turned about. He lost and kept on losing. He couldn't take in what was happening, he was down to his last twenty pounds. 'That's me, I'm out,' he said.

'Easy lad, we'll take your marker, all friends aren't we?' Eddie, he knew the gambler in the younger man couldn't just get up and walk away.

Rab was sweating. He was down £860, how could this have happened?

'One last hand?' Paul suggested. 'I know Mick will vouch for you.' Rab nodded. Ever the gambler, he had to play, he knew his luck was about to change.

'What you got then, Rab? asked Paul.

This time he was sure, he had them. 'A straight flush, ten, nine, eight, seven, six of hearts,' he said as he laid the cards on the table, beaming from ear to ear.

Paul looked Rab straight in the eyes and then laid out his cards, a Royal Flush. 'Hard luck lad.'

'How the fu...' Rab protested.

'Now, now, don't be a sore loser,' said Eddie, 'all's fair in love and poker.'

The last hand dealt had got out of control, the stakes were constantly upped. Rab was in debt for the better part of seven thousand pounds.

'Give the lad a drink, he looks as if he could use one,' Paul said as he folded the cards and stood up from the table. Rab, still sitting, paled, a cold sweat trickling down his spine. 'What we gonna do now, Rab, seven grand's a lot of money?' He walked around the back of the young man and rested both hands on Rab's shoulders.

Rab shuddered as the fingers squeezed - tightly. 'Might take a bit of time, but I'll pay you back,' he said, daring not to move.

'That's the problem - we haven't got the time.' The tone was menacing.

'I'm good for it, Paul, you know that.' Rab was sweating; he could feel it cold running down the centre of his back. And where the hell had Mick had got to when he needed him?

'Rab lad, I don't know you from bleedin Adam. If I let you walk out of here that'll be the last I'll see of you and my seven grand - so, you stay here until I get the money.'

'How the fuck can I get you the cash if you won't let me leave?' Rab protested, still fixed into the chair.

'You just sit here and enjoy your pint while I tell you how we're going to solve your problem. They tell me your old man is worth a bob or two, that right?' Rab nodded. 'Well, in that case I don't see a problem - do you?' Rab rolled his shoulders as Paul released the pressure. He had a vision of his father going ballistic when he found out what he'd done. 'Eddie, get us some more drinks while I tell this little shit how it's going to work.'

Rab couldn't believe what had happened, it was classic they way he'd been drawn in and suckered, after all, hadn't he done the same thing himself?

Chapter 4

Rab was seriously getting worried left alone in the back room of the pub. Christ, he didn't know what to do next. He needed a piss, but daren't leave his seat. His mind was all over the place. What if this? What if that? Maybe he would just stand up, call their bluff and walk out of the pub. It was stupid to think such a thing, he knew he'd never reach the door. Paul and Eddie came into the back room. He wished to hell he had never heard of the bloody *Blacksmiths Arms*.

'Come on, lad, on your feet,' Paul grabbed him by the arm. Rab struggled and tried to shrug him off as he was hoisted up out of the chair.

'Where are you taking me? Let go of me, you wanker,' Rab protested, pulling back against the hand as he was led out through the now empty bar, and through the front door of the pub. As the night air entered his lungs, his legs felt unsteady, light headed he wanted to be sick. He was half pissed. Eddie on one side and Paul on the other he was marched away into the darkness. He was scared, more scared than he had ever been before in his life. Then he felt the warm piss running down his legs.

'Not going far.' Eddie gripped Rab's elbow.

'Shit,' Rab winced with pain as the grip tightened and tried to shake him off.

23

Eddie relaxed the grip a little. 'Fucking wimp.'

'There's no need for any of this, if you let me call my old man we can sort this, he'll pay up.'

'Well, that's one option,' Paul said.

Rab was officially worried.

He was led down a series of narrow cobbled streets, between tall red brick eighteenth century buildings. Overhead the full moon cast long shadows between the high brick walls. He didn't know exactly where they were, but he guessed they were not too far away from the river front. All manner of questions went through Rab's head as he was manhandled through the dark quiet streets. He was sobering quickly. His mind was working overtime, were they going to hurt him? What if his old man didn't pay, what then? Would they just let him go - of course they would once his Dad paid up - he would pay up wouldn't he? He had another thought, an uneasy one, how *could* they just let him walk away? After all, he knew who they were. And where the hell had Mick disappeared to? Questions - his mind was full of them. Then an unexpected opportunity arose, Eddie tripped over an uneven pavement slab.

'Shit,' Eddie fell arse over elbow into the gutter, releasing the grip on Rab's arm as he went down. 'Think I've twisted my ankle.'

Rab knew this was the one and only chance he was going to get. He didn't hesitate, did an about turn and legged it as fast as he could down a narrow alleyway between an engineer's workshop and a scrap yard, Paul and Eddie's scrap yard.

'You little sod,' Paul shouted after him as he reached to help Eddie to his feet. 'I'm alright, mate, go get the little bugger,' he said, picking himself up out of the gutter and hopping on one foot.

Rab continued running down the narrow passage. A wire mesh link fence on one side and a high brick wall the other, he could hear Paul following. A dog barked a "big dog bark" in the scrap yard. Rab could hear the animal growling deeply and dragging its chain as it tried to reach the fence. Startled, he risked a look over his shoulder, he stumbled and bounced off the brick wall, the pain in his shoulder bloody hurt. 'Oh shit, don't let that bloody chain snap.' He had no idea where the alley led to. He pounded on down the narrow alley, panting, his breath heavy. A hundred metres further on he emerged into an open space, a sign on the wall said St James Square. Which way? Left or right? He chose right, hoping he was heading towards the Marina. He stopped to look over his shoulder, took a deep breath and ran on - he'd lost them. If Rab only had known the area a little better, he was only yards away from the *Vauxhall Tavern*.

'He can't be too far away,' Paul said into the mobile, 'not many places to hide when he gets into the open.' He put the mobile in his jeans pocket.

Paul was right, there was nowhere to hide. Rab kept running, crouching low trying to conceal himself behind a line of parked cars. He dropped to his knees and listened, nothing, just the sounds of the night and his own laboured breathing. Then, beneath the vehicles he saw a pair of boots approaching and cursed to himself, he knew he had no chance of escape.

'There you are, you little tosser,' Paul said as he came around the front end of a Vauxhall Corsa. Rab tried to rise to his feet, he'd decide to give it one more go and make a run for it, he had to. 'Whoa,' Paul swung a boot and kicked him in the ankle and Rab went down like a bag of shit. He reached down and grabbed the prostrate youth by his throbbing ankle and unceremoniously dragged him backwards. With his free hand he took out the mobile and pressed the keys. 'Got him, bring the car around to Jimmies Square, I don't want the little twat doing another runner.'

'For fuck's sake, just let me go, I'll get your money, I won't say a word to anyone what's gone on.'

'Just shut it, will you?'

A few short minutes later, Eddie drove up in a Fiat "Rust Bucket". Eddie climbed out and limped around the vehicle, his ankle throbbing. He opened the rear door of the Fiat. Paul hoisted Rab to his feet by the scruff of his shirt collar and brusquely bundled him into the back seats of the Fiat, then climbed in after him.

'Right, let's get him to the lockup before he tries to do another Houdini.'

Rab sat in the rear seats of the car, he was more frightened than ever. He was driven a short way through the narrow cobbled streets to a run-down industrial unit, adjacent to the scrap yard owned by Paul and Eddie. Rab looked up at the three storey dilapidated building through the car window.

Eddie hobbled around to the near side and opened the car door. 'Out,' he grabbed Rab roughly by the top of his arm and pulled him from the car. He didn't resist, it was pointless trying.

He was scared, double scared, dreading what would happen once he was inside. Paul took a bunch of keys from his pocket and unlocked the large heavy wooden sliding door. He grunted with the effort as the doors squeaked and scraped in the metal track, it had been a while since they were last opened. He made a mental note to grease the track. Rab heard rats scurry to the corners as the door opened, he looked to Paul for empathy.

'Don't worry, they're vegetarians.'

They laughed. Rab didn't join in.

Paul reached around the corner of the door and switched on a dim bulb hanging from a flex in the high ceiling. The young gambler was led through what looked to have been a motorcycle workshop in a previous life. His head turned one way, then the other scanning the room, watched by several pairs of eyes in furry velvet suits. Another door was unlocked, a string - pull pulled and another dim bulb struggled to illuminate a self contained room. Eddie put his large hand in the centre of his back and shoved him inside. Rab just stood in the centre of the space bewildered.

Paul gestured with open arms. 'Toilet, fully fitted kitchenette, complete with microwave oven,' he was sounding like a cheap estate agent trying to sell the place. 'Not that you will be using it - but never mind you won't be here long, just 'till your old man coughs up the readies. Oh, and let's not forget the bedroom,' he pointed to an uncomfortable looking single bed in the corner of the room. 'I've spent some very nice evenings here.'

Throughout the one sided conversation, Rab stood looking around the room, no windows just plasterboard covered walls decorated with posters of heavy metal bands and topless page three girls. Gobsmacked he wondered how the hell he'd let himself get into this situation. He knew the answer, greed, pure greed.

'The beauty of this room is it's soundproof.'

Rab looked questioningly. 'Soundproof, why does it need to be soundproof?' He imagined himself screaming and no one hearing.

'Paul had it done when we had the band.'

'Band?' Rab echoed.

'Yeah, a practise room we did a bit of rockabilly. We weren't any good like - it didn't last.' Paul said nostalgically.

'Anyway, you just sit down, there's just one more thing we've got to do.' Rab didn't argue as he was pushed towards the manky mattress on the bed and sat on the edge of the bed. He lifted his head to speak, then changed his mind, his mouth opened and closed. What was the point of protesting? Then out of the blue - whack, Eddie's shovel-like fist smashed into Rab's nose. The cartilage snapped, blood and mucus ran freely down Rab's face and over his T-shirt.

'What... what the... fu...' he mumbled, as he fell back on the bed, holding both hands to his face sobbing, blood running through his fingers. 'Why di...'

'Just shut it, here,' Paul passed the young gambler a dirty stained rag. Rab eased himself back into the sitting position and held the rag to his face; he was in shock and couldn't get a grasp of what was happening. 'Take your T-shirt off.' Paul passed over a sweatshirt to replace the bloody T-shirt.

'Piss off,' he said bravely as he sobbed.

'If you don't want Eddie to give you another smack I'd do as you're told,' Paul told him threateningly.

Rab looked from one man to the other, he didn't doubt Eddie would use his fist again. He took off the T-shirt, his shoulder that pounded the wall ached like buggery. He wiped his shirt across his face, then threw it to the floor and struggled into the sweatshirt, bad shoulder first, easing it over his bloody face and then picked the rag up again. 'Why did you do that? You'll get your money.' He was still sobbing. Holding the dirty rag to his face as he edged backwards up the bed trying to put distance between himself and the fist.

'Aye, I know we'll get the money. I could say I'm sorry about your nose, but I'd be lying. See we've got to make things look realistic. When your old man gets the T-shirt through his letter-box with a ransom note he'll shit himself.'

'Ransom note?'

'That's what I said.'

'You've only got to ask my old man and he'll give you the seven grand.'

'Who said anything about seven grand? I reckon you're worth a bit more than that to him.'

'Yeah, but... I mean...' he dabbed his nose gently.

'Oh, stop the fucking whinging,' Eddie shouted, 'if you weren't so bleeding greedy you wouldn't be in this situation.'

'Steady up, Eddie, give the lad a break,' Paul said playing the "good guy".

'That's what I have done - his bleedin nose.' Only Eddie laughed.

'Was... M... Mick in on this? He managed to splurt out between sobs.'

'Maybe – maybe not.'

Rab was struggling to keep himself from bursting out in a full blown flood of tears. What had started as a game of poker between mates had now turned into his worst nightmare, a nightmare he didn't know when or how it would end.

'Right then, Rab, we're off, you'll be safe tucked up in here. Like we said its pointless shouting, cos no fucker will hear you. We'll be back in the morning with some scran and a coffee.' Paul and Eddie moved to the door. 'Night night, sleep tight, mind the rats don't bite.' The door was slammed shut and the lock turned.

'You'll never get away with this you wankers,' he yelled through the closed door. Rab curled up on the bed, bleeding and feeling afraid - very afraid.

Chapter 5

Marlowe had every intention of enjoying the peace and quiet of North Yorkshire, savouring pints of fine ale in the hostelries of Robin Hoods Bay and Sandsend. He thought maybe he and Archie would venture inland as far as Goathland, home of the fictional television series *Heartbeat* set in the 1960s.

Following a bracing walk along the cliff top in the invigorating autumn wind, Marlowe took off his woollen Hull City hat and stuffed it in his pocket. Then he and Archie took up their place in the *Duke of York* public house with its paintings of the old whaling ships on the walls. With a view of the River Esk running into the harbour the pair sat at a beaten copper topped table. Thanks to the brisk cliff top walk, he had built up an appetite, he was going to enjoy the platter of fresh Whitby Scampi and chips on the table before him. He always enjoyed his food, especially when he didn't have to prepare it himself. Even more when it was washed down with a pint of brewed in the cask Real Ale. With his meal finished Marlowe walked across to the bar. 'Put another one in there, please,' he asked the barman pushing his glass across the bar top, along with a five pound note.

He watched as the ale from the hand-pump swirled in the glass. 'Cheers,' he said, pocketing his change and admiring the sparkling dark liquid.

'How long you got left?' Asked the barman, as he wiped down the Mahogany top with a towel.

'Ten days or so before it's back to the grind,' Marlowe replied, resting his elbows on the bar hoping for a conversation. There was only so much conversation he could have with Archie.

'What is it again you do for a living?' asked the barman.

'I'm a copper.' The barman raised an eyebrow - end of conversation, he suddenly found an urgent job that needed attending to at the other end of the bar

Marlowe returned to his table with his pint, thinking how strange it was the way some folk reacted when he told them his occupation. But it was "water off a duck's back", it wasn't the first time it happened and it definitely wouldn't be the last.

Then the inevitable happened, he knew it would - his mobile sang out the Beatles "Paperback Writer". He reached in his jacket pocket, took out the mobile and checked the display screen. It was Detective Inspector Dave Gowan, his second in command back at the nick. He accepted the call.

'You just couldn't leave me in peace could you? This better be good, Dave,' he said into the handset.

'Yeah, well, sorry to interrupt your break, but I thought you'd like to know, unless you know already.'

'Know what?' He answered as he glanced out of the window overlooking the harbour watching the tide come in.

'I take it you haven't heard then?'

'Come on, Dave, get on with it my pint's going flat,' he said as he reached under the table and patted Archie.

'It's about "Shag Pile Charlie".'

He was referring to Charles Bacuss, the carpet salesman, the man who had stolen Marlowe's wife - sort of. The following divorce had left him strapped for cash and having to rethink his finances. Consequently Marlowe had taken up residency on board the *Daisy*, a seventy foot long, narrow-boat moored along the Beck in the market town of Beverley.

'Passed away has he? I'll send some flowers.' Marlowe replied sarcastically as he picked up his pint and sipped.

'Unfortunately not - it's his lad, he's gone missing.'

'So, pass it on to Missing Persons, hardly comes within our remit does it?' Marlowe sipped again, he didn't like the sound of the way the conversation was going.

'Looks like he might have been kidnapped...' He never finished the sentence.

'You're winding me up surely.' Funny - the ale now had a foul taste.

'Straight up, Phil, it seems he's been missing for two days. Now a packet, and a sort of ransom note have been shoved through their letter-box.

Marlowe turned towards the window and lowered his voice. 'What was in the packet?'

'It was a padded envelope containing a T-shirt covered in blood, along with a note saying "We'll be in touch".'

'Trust that bloody woman! She can still manage to ruin my holiday. Have you informed Superintendent Bulmer?'

'Not yet, didn't know how you would want to play this.'

'Okay, let's keep this in house for the time being. Give me time to get sorted out here and I'll come straight to the nick. If anything develops in the meantime, give me a bell.' He hung up, cursing "Shag Pile Charlie" *and* his son, also muttering a few choice words about his ex-wife, Karen.

Chapter 6

Marlowe, with Archie pulling on his lead made his way back along Church Lane to his rented accommodation. 'Bloody woman,' he said selfishly to Archie, who didn't take a blind bit of notice, standing there wagging his tail as Marlowe unlocked the front door to the cottage.

It didn't take long to gather up their belongings and stuff them into his holdall. Half an hour after receiving the call his bag was in the boot of his Ford Mondeo and the pair were heading along the coast road towards Hull. He'd managed less than three whole days leave without interruption, he should have known his holiday's were usually jinxed. The best he could hope for was that it was just some stupid student prank - they'd happened before. God help Dave Gowan if it was.

The A171 coast road from Whitby to Scarborough isn't the best road in the world, twisting and turning it skirts the edge of the desolate moors and the North Sea cliffs. Marlowe cursed, he knew he should have taken the less direct, but faster route across the North Yorkshire Moors via Pickering and Malton. He razzed to himself as he followed a 1960s vintage tractor for mile after mile. 'Pull in you selfish sod,' he yelled to the driver who was oblivious to the fact he was causing a half mile tailback of traffic. A journey that should have taken around an hour and a half, took just over two hours.

Marlowe eventually drove his Mondeo into the Gordon Street Police Station car park, only to find his allotted parking space had been taken by DI Dave Gowan's Audi.

He double parked, opened the car door and Archie immediately jumped free and peed up against Gowan's Audi. Serves you right, you bugger he thought as he climbed out from the car. 'Hope they haven't changed the security code,' he said to Archie, as he punched the number into the lock of the station rear door. It hadn't been changed, he had hardly been away long enough.

'Well, well, well, I thought you weren't back until next week?' Desk Sergeant Trevor Cleeves said as the DCI walked into the custody area. Cleeves himself had only recently returned to work after suffering a heart attack whilst on duty, brought about by the stress of the job - amongst other things.

'So did I, Trev, but you know me the bad penny. When did you start back?'

'This morning, just doing a bit part-time, doctor's orders and all that.'

'You're looking a lot better since the last time I saw you in Castle Hill.'

The Castle Hill Hospital in the nearby village of Cottingham has one of the best Cardiac Care Units in the country.

'Yeah, I'm on the mend now. Must say I'm glad to be back even if it is part-time, I was getting bored out of my mind.'

'You've lost a bit of weight as well.'

Cleeves patted his round stomach. 'That's what hospital food does for you!'

'I need a favour, Trevor, you wouldn't look after Archie for a bit would you?' Marlowe held out Archie's lead.

'I should bloody coco, this is a nick not the RSPCA,' and promptly turned about busying himself, a big grin on his face with his back to the DCI

'Arse,' said Marlowe deliberately loud enough for Cleeves to hear.

'I heard that Magnum, and the answer is still no.' Marlowe and Cleeves had been friends since school. Cleeves had always played on the DCI's name Philip Marlowe, who had unfortunately been named after Raymond Chandler's fictional private detective.

'Can't you just put him in a cell until I get sorted?' Marlowe almost pleaded.

'And just what will I put on the charge sheet? Arrested for peeing in the car park?'

'You could do, he took a leak up the back wheel of Dave Gowan's Audi.'

'Give him here, and don't be long, it'll be Sod's Law the Super will pay us one of his surprise visits.'

'Cheers, Trev, you're a pal,' Marlowe led Archie around the desk.

'I know I am, and don't forget where he is!' He took a hold of the lead and led Archie through the back. 'Who's a good boy then? Let's see if we can find you a biscuit.' Marlowe heard Cleeves say when they were out of sight.

Cleeves came over as an obstructive sod - but it was all for show.

'Wasn't expecting to see you back, boss. Have a good time?' DC Lee Kristianson asked as he lifted his eyes from the computer screen.

'And I wasn't expecting to be back.'

'You had a good time, though?'

'Hmm. Where's the DI?' Marlowe asked, as he walked over to the white board to see if there were any late additions.

'About somewhere.'

'Find him, will you? I'll be in the office.' Marlowe went into his glass cubicle, hung up his coat and settled behind his desk. He checked his watch, 4pm, he didn't intend on being in the station any longer than he had to, after all he was officially still on leave. He automatically switched on the computer, then, ping, ping, ping; email after email filled the screen. 'Bugger this,' he said out loud and turned the machine off. He sat back in his chair with his hands behind his head and closed his eyes - sore after his long drive.

'Knock, knock.' DI Dave Gowan walked in accompanied by Detective Sergeant Jenny Bright. 'Sorry about cutting your holiday short, boss, but I thought you'd want to know what was happening. You know - with it being Shag Pile's lad and all that.' Gowan passed across the folder he was holding.

'Have I *got* to *read* this?' Asked Marlowe as he glanced at his watch again. 'I am officially still on my jollies *as* you well know,' he dropped the file onto the desk and pushed it towards Jenny. Marlowe gestured for them to sit. 'When you're ready.'

'Right,' Gowan started on the run down of events, 'it appears Robert hasn't been seen, or heard of since Sunday 16th October.'

'And it's now?' Marlowe looked at the desk calendar '... the 18th, two days and we're sure that was the last anyone saw of him?'

'From what we're led to believe.'

'What about the family?'

'According to his mother...' Marlowe looked up quickly, 'correction, step-mother the last time he made contact was Sunday lunch time.'

'What sort of contact, phone, email, what?'

'He went to the house to borrow some cash from her a couple of days prior and on Sunday went to pay it back before his father found out,' Jenny answered.

'What did he want the money for?'

'He told her he needed some study material.'

'Yeah, right,' Marlowe said sceptically. 'What about the T-shirt, how was it delivered?'

'By hand, someone shoved it through their letter-box in the early hours of the morning, it was on the doormat when they came downstairs. It's with forensics as we speak.' Gowan reached across, opened the folder and took out a sheet of paper. 'This is a copy of the note that was in with the T-shirt.' Gowan read out the brief message. "Don't get the police involved, we will be in touch".

'Short and sweet. So I take it you're not thinking it's some sort of prank? We're taking it seriously?'

Dave Gowan raised his eyebrows at the suggestion.

'To be honest, boss, from the amount of blood on the T-shirt, well...'

'Just asking - students and all that.' Marlowe sat forward in his chair, resting his elbows on the desk.

'What's the state of play so far?'

'Jenny went around to see the family as soon as the call came in, you know with it being Sha... Bacuss. Mr and Mrs Bacuss are coming in first thing in the morning.'

'So, Jenny, how did Bacuss come across?'

'Frantic, he had no idea who could be behind it or why anyone would want to kidnap Robert. By the way Mrs Bacuss sends her regards.'

'Hmm,' it wasn't worthy of a response.

'Boss, I've no need to tell you we'll be running short handed on this. And we're still a DS down.'

'I *am* aware we're down a DS, Dave and I will do my best to get it sorted. What about friends at the university?'

'It doesn't look like he had many.'

'Has, you mean has.'

'Yeah, right.'

'Okay, I'll call around and see Shag... Bacuss on my way home. I agree we treat this as a kidnap until we know otherwise.' Almost as an afterthought he asked.'We have done a trace on his mobile?'

'Turned off or flat battery, either way its not registering on the network.' Jenny told him.

Visiting Bacuss was the last thing Marlowe wanted to do, but he knew he had no real choice in the matter but make a personal appearance. It wasn't as if Marlowe didn't like the man - he despised him.

Home to Shag Pile Charlie, or Charles Bacuss as it was stated on his birth certificate and Karen, Marlowe's ex, was a large 1980's detached property set in half an acre of landscaped gardens in Cottingham, a large village on the north west edge of the city. During the drive Marlowe couldn't help but reflect on past events - he often did. He didn't really blame Bacuss for ruining his marriage he'd done a good job of that one himself. The marriage was on the way to being over long before the carpet salesman came on the scene. He was merely the catalyst that brought it to a head. The truth of the matter lay in too many late nights at the nick and the pub and not enough time at home. The only good thing to come out of the divorce was that Marlowe was given custody of Archie, whom the ex-Mrs Marlowe always said, "you love that dog more than you do me". He didn't argue that one in the divorce court.

The Mondeo tyres crunched on the deep gravel as he drove around the circular drive and pulled up directly opposite the front pillared door, like something out of a posh magazine. Karen and Charles promptly appeared, looking harassed. Charles still managed to look dapper, as always, still wearing a broad pin stripe three piece business suit worth more than Marlowe's monthly salary. Karen, wearing expensive looking designer jeans and loose fitting T-shirt, looked stressed. Funny, thought Marlowe, she'd never been that materialistic when they were married - then again, they'd never had money to spare

For a moment or two Marlowe contemplated as to whether he should leave Archie in the car - should he or shouldn't he? No contest. 'Come on, pal,' he said and Archie jumped out through the open car door, ran straight to one of the concrete pillars and cocked his leg.

'Sorry about that.'

'No worries, Phil. It's good of you to come yourself,' said Bacuss as he walked towards Marlowe with an out-stretched arm to shake his hand.

'All part of the service, Charles,' he replied as he reluctantly shook the offered hand. Karen stood on the doorstep, waiting.

'You're looking well, Karen, considering,' he said as he was ushered into the house. She looked at Archie giving a slightly disapprovingly look, but didn't say anything as the dog bounded in before them. After the divorce, on the odd occasion when he was feeling nostalgic, Marlowe had driven past the house, even stopping at the entrance to their drive. But this was the first time he had actually been inside. Envy would be the best way to describe Marlowe's feelings as he walked into the wide hallway. He looked to the left, through the open doorway, it looked like the dining room. Karen waited, holding open the door to the right and then smiled as she stood aside to let him enter the sitting room. This room alone could have swallowed up the *Daisy* from stem to stern.

'No need to stand on ceremony, Phil.' Bacuss gestured towards the expensive looking Chesterfield sofa.

Pompous pratt he wanted to say - but didn't.

'Tea, coffee?' Karen asked as Marlowe took a seat on the sofa and almost sank into the deep cushions.

'Tea please, you couldn't get a drink for Archie could you?' Karen went through to the kitchen with the dog at her heels, although she didn't like the mutt, she wished it no harm.

Bacuss remained standing, a trait he'd developed when dealing with customers - looking down on people.

'Ok, Charles, let's start at the beginning?' Marlowe settled back on the expensive sofa trying not to feel conspicuous in his cheap suit.

'We've already been through this with DS Bright,' he said still standing.

'And I'd like to hear it first hand for myself,' pausing, then adding 'please.' Karen came back with Marlowe's tea and sat down next to him - but not too close. 'Thanks, when you're ready.'

'There's very little to say really, we didn't know anything was amiss until the T-shirt business. I'd rang Robert's mobile prior to its arrival - to see if he was still shunning me, the call went straight to voice mail, I assumed he was ignoring the call.'

'Is that usual?'

'When he sees it's me who's calling, yes. That is, unless he's after some cash. Anyway, with the T-shirt arriving, I rang the police when he didn't pick up.'

'When and who was the last to speak to Robert?'Marlowe looked from one to the other.

'That would be me,' said Karen, 'around Sunday lunchtime.'

'On the phone?'

'No, he came round to drop off some money he borrowed.'

'Nothing seemed to be bothering him?'

Karen fiddled with a gold bracelet on her wrist. 'No, not in the least, he was fine.'

'Did he often borrow money?'

'No, not really, he usually asked his father, but the situation being as it was.'

'Situation?'

'Yes,' she looked toward her husband.

Bacuss cleared his throat. 'Robert and I haven't been getting on too well lately.'

'Anyway, he said he needed the money for books, then Saturday morning he rang and he said he'd managed to get some second-hand ones and wouldn't be needing the money after all. He called around late Sunday morning to pay me back.' Karen looked to Charles and back to Marlowe. 'I told him to keep it anyway, but he insisted I have it, especially after the row he'd had with his father.'

'A row?' Marlowe directed the question to Charles, who walked across to the drinks cabinet, poured himself a generous single malt whisky from an expensive looking bottle and held the glass up to Marlowe. 'No thanks... you were about to say?'

'We'd had words, once again.' Charles offered, emphasising on the *again*. 'I stopped his allowance for wasting money, told him it was about time he started to act like a grown up and fend for himself.' He remained standing as he sipped from the cut glass tumbler. Marlowe reckoned he liked looking down on people, maybe he thought it gave him some kind of edge.

'And he wasn't happy I'm thinking?'

'Too true, he was bloody fuming, called me a greedy old bastard and stormed out. Haven't seen him since.'

'But this was before the last time you spoke to him, Karen?'

'Yes, all this happened a couple of weeks back, as I've said he came around Sunday and things seemed fine.

'Just one more question tonight, what on earth is Robert doing, living in a student flat when he has a perfectly good home within easy distance of the University?'

'Simple,' said Charles, 'he wanted to "taste" life and live like a real student. I was paying the bills for his apartment of course. Consequently, when we'd had our words, I told him straight, if that's how he wanted to live his life, then that's how it would be from now on, he could bloody well fend for himself and pay for his own accommodation.'

Marlowe stood up and passed the cup and saucer to Karen. 'Thanks. As soon as we know anything I'll be in touch. I'd like you to come into the station first thing to make a statement, I'll have a car pick you up.'

'That won't be necessary.'

No, you won't want to be seen in squad car Marlowe wanted to say, but held his tongue.

'In the meantime, if you remember or hear anything, phone the station right away, okay?'

'Thanks for coming, Phil,' said Charles as he walked Marlowe to the front door.

'Least I could do,' he said as they shook hands, Marlowe slyly wiped his hand down the side of his trousers

'Just get my lad back.'

Marlowe replied with just a nod. 'See you later, Karen,' he shouted over his shoulder adding, 'unfortunately' under his breath as he walked towards the car. 'Archie, come on.' The dog ran to the car and jumped in through the open door. Marlowe thought he'd done well, keeping his personal differences in check as there was no love lost between him and Bacuss, or Karen for that matter. But needs must, a job's a job and has to be done professionally, no matter personal differences - or so he told the members of his team.

As he pulled out of the Bacuss's drive he looked at the dashboard clock, it was nearly 6.00pm, it had been a long day and he was knackered. Only a few hours ago, he had been taking in the fresh air along the North Yorkshire coast cliff tops. It was a far cry from sampling good food and fine ale without a care in the world. Right now he was looking forward to getting back home.

The *Daisy* had been painted in the traditional bright colours, red, blue and yellow. Some of the flower tubs on the upper saloon roof still had a few flowers in late bloom. After the divorce settlement the floating home was all he could comfortably afford without putting himself in debt with a massive mortgage, and that was something he wasn't going to do so late in life. The boat was more than adequate for his needs, connected to the main services on the quayside and equipped with all the mod-cons, even if they were miniature in size to be accommodated aboard his floating home.

With his holiday cut short and no time for shopping for fresh food, it was back to the single copper's friends, the microwave and freezer. That posed the next question, was there anything *in* the freezer? He was lucky, if you could call a frozen lasagne lucky. He removed it from the wrapper, pierced the film lid, placed it the microwave oven and zapped it. With a glass of Australian Merlot in front of him, he sat in the small saloon and waited for the ping.

Ten minutes later, he sat in the dinette area of the *Daisy's* lounge with his dinner in front of him, as he watched the local news on the television. It was as if he had never been away, back to the routine. Once dinner was finished, if a frozen meal eaten out of the container could be called dinner the long day began to catch up with him. He could feel the autumn wind gathering strength, as it blew along the Beck gently rocking the *Daisy* on her moorings. Still with his slippers on he reached for his jacket, made sure his cigarettes and lighter were in his pocket and shouted for Archie. 'Come on matey, a quick fag before bedtime, I reckon we should have an early night.' He clipped on the flexi-lead that allowed Archie to do dog things in the long grass of the river bank. As he sat on a concrete mooring bollard along the Beckside, he could feel the biting edge of the wind finding its way inside the jacket. He shivered a little as he mulled things over, his past life with Karen, and Shag Pile Charlie's part in his downfall. He knew it was his own fault the marriage had fallen apart, something he couldn't deny, but all the same it was good having someone to blame.

Chapter 7

A good night's sleep was unusual for Marlowe, over recent months he had developed the habit of falling asleep on the *Daisy's* dinette seating, more often than not waking with a stiff back and aching joints. He put it down to the sea air and a change of scenery that he woke early feeling refreshed, and ready to take on what the day could throw at him, even if it did involve Karen and Bacuss. Marlowe went through to the galley, filled the kettle and turned it on, he had just enough time to freshen up while the kettle boiled. Integral to his bedroom - the only bedroom, was the *Daisy's* small but functional shower cubicle. Standing below the cascading power shower, he felt the tension in his muscles, ease as the hot water washed over him, next he shaved, dressed in his work clothes and made breakfast - a mug of tea in the galley followed by a smoke sitting on the towpath bollard while Archie did his own toiletries.   He locked the hatch on the *Daisy* and secured Archie in his pen, to await the arrival of Harry, his adoptive guardian. Forty five minutes after waking he was driving down the towpath heading to the nick.

The DCI had been stationed at the West Hull, Gordon Street Police Station just off the Boulevard for the past two years. Prior to this posting he had been stationed at the old headquarters on Queen's Gardens in the city centre. Marlowe was an old fashioned copper, he didn't give much thought to office politics, he played the game just enough to allow him to reach his current rank and he was happy with that. That's not saying he hadn't pissed one or two people off along the way, hence his transfer to an inner city station. At first he was a little aggrieved with the transfer, now he thought differently, he was left alone to run the CID department how he wanted it run. Leading from the front and getting his hands dirty was a big bonus.

Even though he had set off before the rush hour the traffic was heavy as he reached the city, bumper to bumper for the majority of the way down Beverley Road. He was pleased with himself for not giving in to his usual bout of road rage - after all he was going to have to deal with Shag Pile and that was enough for any man.

'Morning Poirot,' Sergeant Trevor Cleeves said cheerfully as Marlowe entered the nick from the rear car park.

I will not rise to Trevor's piss taking he said to himself. 'Morning Trev,' he replied jovially, trying his best to avoid getting into an early morning battle of banter with his old friend.

Cleeves knew which buttons to press to get the DCI going. 'On your own this morning then?' he looked around and past Marlowe, searching for his four legged companion.

'Aye, just me. Archie's safe in his compound waiting for Harry to collect him.'

Harry and his wife Joyce lived in the Old Lock Keepers cottage further down the Beverley Beck tow-path. Since Marlowe had taken residence in his floating home, the retired couple had become good friends and neighbours, taking a firm liking to both Marlowe and Archie. Joyce was always there with a nourishing meal when he was in need. She had an uncanny sense and always produced a home cooked meal at the right time. While Harry, a retired sheet metal worker did whatever odd job that needed taking care of on the *Daisy*. If the truth was known, Harry looked forward to the respite from domestic "bliss", and also took Archie for long walks down the towpath and over the neighbouring fields.

'So, Shag Pile's lad then?' Cleeves said, speaking to Marlowe's back as he walked through the custody area.

Marlowe stopped in his tracks. With his back to Cleeves he held up "the hand", to stop the conversation before it could escalate into a slanging match.

'I haven't been back off leave for five minutes, Trev, I'm not in the mood for piss taking.'

'Me, take the piss? DCI Marlowe you offend me,' he replied, trying to sound affronted, 'well, maybe,' he smiled to himself.

'Might have known you wouldn't be able to resist having a go,' Marlowe said as he turned around. 'Give me a few minutes to get sorted then come through - and I'll have a coffee, milk no sugar,' he disappeared before the Sergeant could respond with some sarcastic remark, like make your own bloody coffee. Marlowe opened the squad room door with an exaggerated flourish. 'Good morning, one and all.'

He was met with the early morning grunts and groans. 'Good morning to you too, boss,' he replied to himself.

'Oh, morning, boss. Thought you were still on holiday, boss?' DC Tanya Etherington said, looking up from her keyboard.

'Yes, Tanya, so did I. Any idea where the DI is?'

'He's with Jenny... DS Bright, they were in early. Think they went for a coffee,' she replied with a touch of envy.

'It's alright for some. Go and drag them back will you, tell them as quick as they like.'

DC Lee Kristianson smiled, he was usually the one the boss sent on errands. 'And be quick about it,' Lee said to Tanya's back.

'I heard that, constable,' Marlowe shouted through the open door, smiling to himself. Detective Constable Lee Kristianson was the newest member of the team, rising from the Gordon Street uniform ranks. He could be a lazy sod at times, but he had the makings of a good detective.

Tanya was correct in her assumption. Dave and Jenny where indeed one floor up in the station canteen.

'The boss was a bit pissed off being dragged back off his holiday,' Jenny said as she picked up her cup of herbal tea.

'Not surprised, wouldn't you be?' Gowan said as he put the last of his bacon roll in his mouth. 'Especially if it was anything to do with your ex and her new spouse. Let's be honest, if I hadn't told him he'd have gone ballistic when he did find out,' Gowan said smiling.

'Talking about ex-wives has your divorce come through yet?'

'Signed the papers and sent them back - day before yesterday.' The smile was gone. 'Just got to wait for the decree what's its name to come through.'

'Nisi,' she told him. 'That explains why you were a bit arsey the last day or so.'

Gowan just shrugged his shoulders. 'Arsey, me?' he tried to sound offended. 'Once its rubber stamped I can move on.'

'What about the kids?' asked Jenny genuinely interested.

'Sorted, I can see them when I want - no problem there. Saying that, if that witch of a mother in-law had her way she'd never let me see them. I reckon if it wasn't for the old cow we'd have been able to work it out, probably still be together, but hey ho, that's life.'

'Sir, Sarge, sorry to interrupt,' Tanya said as she approached their table. 'The boss is asking for you - poste haste, if you know what I mean.' Tanya's eyes locked onto a piece of toast on Jenny's plate. 'You eating that, Sarge?' She shook her head. 'I missed breakfast, is it all right?' she looked longingly at the half a slice of buttered toast.

'Help yourself.'

'Thanks.' Tanya picked up the toast and left.

'No prizes for guessing what this'll be about,' Dave said as he pushed his empty mug into the centre of the table. 'You ready?'

'Do you know the bosses-ex?' Jenny asked as they walked back to the squad room.

'I met her a couple of times at Christmas parties and the like. To be honest, I prefer Archie's company, he's more amenable and house trained.' They both laughed.

'I'm still hungry,' Gowan said as they walked out of the canteen.

'You should have grabbed that piece of toast when you had the chance.'

'Come on, best go and see what the PI has to say,' Gowan said leading the way down the stairs.

Behind his back the DCI was often referred to as the PI, yet another play on his name - Philip Marlowe, Private Investigator. Woe betides anyone who called him it within earshot - especially a junior officer.

Chapter 8

Over the past couple of years the interior of the nineteenth century Gordon Street nick had been transformed, bringing it into the 21st Century, whilst the exterior still retained many of the original Victorian features, including the blue lamp above the entrance door. Despite the extensive modernisation of the building, office space at the Gordon Street nick was at a premium. Space had always been a problem, and not one afforded to the DCI. He had been allocated a sectioned off glass cubicle in the main squad room. Marlowe had tried to make the small space more comfortable with a small two seater sofa and some of his own items, but all they did was make the office appear even smaller, more so when half the team was in there.

'Right then,' the DCI said, 'tell me what sort of mess we've got.' He dropped his reading glasses on the desk and sat back in his battered chair, as Gowan and Bright entered the "gold fish bowl".

Jenny sat on the spare chair while Dave Gowan lowered his lanky frame onto the low sofa. Jenny had learned the hard way, "do-not-sit-on-the-sofa-whilst-wearing-a-skirt".

'You mean Shag Pile's lad?' asked Dave.

'There's something else more pressing *is* there Dave?' he asked pointedly. 'And can we please keep an air of professionalism about this and not refer to him as Shag Pile

55

- at least during this investigation?' Marlowe tried very hard not to smile - and failed.

'Well, it's just we've got a lot of stuff on at the moment, thought you might need briefing on the ongoing workload, you being on leave and all that.' Gowan said firmly standing his ground with the DCI.

'First things first, Dave, how long did my leave last? Oh yes, my leave lasted less than forty eight hours,' he said sarcastically. 'You can brief me on the rest once I know where we're going with this. Is this kidnap genuine?' he looked from Dave to Jenny and back again.

'My gut feeling is yes...' Gowan said without qualifying the statement, sinking further into the sofa, his knees nearly up to his chin.

'Jenny, what's your take on this?' The DCI sat forward, resting his elbows on the desk making pyramids with his fingers.

'The same boss, I think it's the real thing.'

'Could it not be some student prank?' Marlowe studied the faces.

There was a knock on the door and Sergeant Cleeves walked in.

'Coffee, Magnum,' he said as he put down a steaming mug. Friends since their school days, Cleeves was the only one who could get away with quips about the DCI's name.

'Cheers, Trevor, park yourself if you can find any room. I've just asked if this could be a student prank rather than an actual crime?'

Cleeves moved a couple of folders and squeezed his arse onto the corner of Marlowe's desk. 'The T-shirt was covered in blood - that's no prank.'

'If the blood is human, for all we know it could have come from the local butcher's shop,' Jenny suggested playing devil's advocate.

'Not so, Jenny, lab reports just come in, it's definitely human, whether it's the lad's or not we won't know until we get the DNA results back.'

'Shit.'

'Language! Sergeant Bright, it doesn't become a lady – but then again, you're no...'

Marlowe cut him short. 'Okay, Trevor, that'll do. Right then, Robert Arthur Bacuss, tell me all,' he said as he picked up his coffee and settled back in his chair.

'As you already know *Mr Bacuss*,' Cleeves emphasised making a point, 'there's no need to elaborate there. The lad's a third year student at Hull Uni, no convictions and he seems a decent lad from all accounts, at this stage I can't tell you anything more. There's been no developments overnight, by that I mean no contact from whoever abducted the lad. The parents, however, did call the station several times during last evening to see if there was any news,' Trevor Cleeves read from an A4 sheet.

'Have a word with Bacuss and get his authorisation for us to record their phone calls, landline and mobiles.' Dave Gowan added it to the growing task list in the A4 log book. 'Jenny, will you sort out a Family Liaison Officer? If we haven't got anybody suitable in-house get someone from Headquarters.'

'Talking about that, shouldn't we be thinking about handing this case over to Serious Crimes?' Jenny said as she brushed her hair away from her face.

'Maybe,' he thought for a moment, then added, 'I'll square it up with Superintendent Bulmer, this is one I want to keep in house if possible.'

'We've already got a team of uniforms canvassing the University campus.' Trevor Cleeves said as he shifted positions on the edge of the desk.

'How long before we get the DNA results back on the T-shirt?' Jenny asked.

'It's been fast tracked by the end of business tomorrow - but as we all know they've said it before,' Dave Gowan said rolling his eyes.

Marlowe slammed his hand on the desk, palm down. 'Right, Jenny, I think you and I will have a ride out and have a look at the lad's flat.'

'Aren't you officially still on leave?' Cleeves had to get in.

'True, Trevor, very true...'

'How does that affect the Health and Safety aspect of things?' Cleeves asked just for the hell of winding Marlowe up.

'I'll give HR a call and tell them I'm officially back, alright? Now can we get on, *please?*'

'Just wanted to make sure we have all options covered...' Cleeves said with a smile.

Marlowe was wise to Cleeves and his windup and cut him short. 'Trevor, finished? You must have some guests to attend too? Thanks for your input, goodbye, Trevor.'

'Right, I'll be off then,' he said, easing himself off the desk corner. 'I knew him when he was a wet behind the ears Plod,' he said to no one and everyone as he left the room, smirking to himself.

'Dave, I'll leave it to you to liaise with Trev on the door to door. Try to keep on his good side and see if we can have some extra bodies if he's got any spare. If not I'll get the Super to draft us some in from elsewhere.'

Chapter 9

In the industrialised part of English Street, not far from the lockup, Paul and Eddie sat having breakfast in *Fat Sam's* greasy spoon. At a tea stained Formica topped table the two sat munching their way through fatty fried breakfasts, described as "The Best Full English In The City", when it should have read within ten metres. Paul had had enough of the artery filling cholesterol and pushed his plate of greasy slop away in favour of his tobacco tin. He pushed his chair back and with nimble fingers rolled a cigarette.

'You sent the T-shirt then?' asked Eddie as he speared a chunk of soggy fat soaked mushroom.

'Better than that, I shoved it through their letter-box meself.' Paul replied as he flicked his lighter and lit his cigarette. Sam the cafe owner, like his customers, didn't bother too much with the no-smoking rule.

'What about fingerprints?'

'C'mon, Eddie, I wore gloves didn't I?'

Grease dripping down Eddie's chin as he spoke. 'You reckon they called the police?' He wiped it clear with the back of his hand. 'Give us another couple of mugs of tea will you, Sam,' he called to the fat man behind the counter.

'We've got to assume they have, they was hardly not going to, no matter what we told 'em.' Paul spat out a loose piece of tobacco onto the floor. 'Gonna give them a call later.'

'Won't the cops be listening to their phone calls?'

'Don't know, maybe - maybe not. I bought a second-hand pay as you go mobile and a few different SIM cards, I'll swap cards when I've made the call.' Sam came over and placed two mugs of steaming tea on the table, their contents spilling onto the table. 'Steady up Sam!' The fat man shrugged his shoulders and walked away lighting his own fag as he went. 'Tosser,' Paul said under his breath. 'I'm thinking fifteen, maybe twenty grand, what do you reckon?'

'Sounds about right. But there is another option,' Eddie said with a smile.

'And what would that be?' Paul asked.

Eddie looked around making sure Sam wasn't in earshot and leaned in closer across the table. 'We sell him,' he said seriously keeping his voice low.

'Fuck off, what would we do - auction him on eBay? Start him off at 99p with no reserve?' Paul laughed at the notion, he'd never heard anything so ludicrous.

'Get serious, Paul, we sell him and get shot. I know a bloke who'd give us a few grand and he'd be off our hands.'

'You're serious aren't you?' Paul wasn't laughing anymore.

'Course I am, we could cut our losses, make a few grand and get it done with.'

'Not sure about that, Eddie, I'll have to think about it.'

'Just sayin that's all, no aggro and few quid in our pockets.' They finished their breakfast in silence. Paul had a lot to think about.

To sell Rab was definitely the easier option, but Paul had a few overheads to take care of, not mentioning the debts that had mounted up leading to the closure of the pub. He needed more than a few grand. But then again?

Setting up the charade to fleece Rab had not come cheap and a few people were queuing up to be paid. Until recently the *Blacksmiths Arms* had belonged to Paul's family. For the past twenty years it had been a family run pub, but with the decline in the nearby industries and a shifting population, the brewery had finally called time along with the bank who had demanded the overdraft be paid off or repossession. Now the pub was up for sale.

If things went according to plan, Paul's deal with young Mick would mean the pub could be brought out of 'retirement'. It was a once in a lifetime opportunity he couldn't let pass, but it had been no easy feat to set up at short notice.

The *Blacksmiths Arms* was to be sold, lock, stock and barrel, except that is for the stock of spirits and wine which Paul removed long before the bank's valuation people did their thing. In other words the pub was still a functioning unit, or would be once Paul and his team had finished the mammoth task of cleaning and re-stocking the main bar. The place was given a thorough clean through; he returned the bottles of spirits to the optics and borrowed a couple of barrels of beer from the landlord of the *White Swan*. The last job was the removal of the *For Sale* sign above the front door. After a solid twenty four hours or so of hard work, the *Blacksmiths Arms* was once again ready to re-open its doors, to one special customer - Robert Arthur Bacuss.

Mick Harrison would get some kind of revenge and a few bob in his pocket, Robert Arthur Bacuss would receive a valuable life lesson and Paul would get his pub back.

'Let me out of here you bastards!' Rab yelled in frustration, knowing full well no one outside the soundproof room could hear him. He had hardly slept for two nights, his eyes sore from crying. Filthy with encrusted blood from his broken nose, he dropped to the bed, picked up the water bottle he'd been given and took a deep swallow then threw the bottle at the wall and sobbed - again. Two days and nights had passed since his incarceration. More than once he thought about whether or not he could overpower Paul and make his escape. He dismissed the idea, he wouldn't stand a chance against the man built like a brick shipyard. He decided he would have to work on another plan, but what?

On the plus side Rab hadn't been left to starve, Paul visited the lockup several times over the previous days to check on the young gambler, bringing with him a take-away of some kind or a burger. Every time the key was turned in the lock, he hoped this would be the day he was set free. This time was no different. Paul slid the bolts and unlocked the door and entered Rab's "cell", locking the door behind him.

Rab stood up to his full height, but still dwarfed by the bigman. 'How much longer are you going to keep me prisoner?' He demanded to know with a trace of bravado in his voice.

'Prisoner, that's stretching it a bit,' Paul said as he walked further into the room.

Rab's bravado disappeared. 'Well, what would you call it? It's hardly a luxury retreat is it?' Rab stepped back a pace, half expecting a slap.

'Calm yourself down. As soon as your old man gets his wallet out, you'll be out of here in double quick time.'

'Wish I could believe that,' he said as he sat on the edge of the bed.

'Believe what you want, now cop for this,' Paul passed across a bacon sandwich he'd bought at the café.

Rab ripped it from the wrapper and bit in ravenously. 'And what has Mick got to do with all this? He asked with a mouthful of food. 'Thought he was my mate?'

'Well, that's mates for yer, you never know where you are with 'em. Now hold this up, I'm gonna take your picture.' Paul passed Rab a copy of the morning paper, with the date outlined in red marker pen. Rab did as he was asked. 'Smile for the camera, well the phone or whatever.' The phone shutter clicked recording the photograph of a bloodied faced Rab holding up the newspaper. 'Your old man might print an enlargement for above the fireplace,' chuckled Paul.

'Seriously, how long do you think you can keep me here?' He threw the newspaper to the floor.

'Oh for Christ's sake play another record will you, you're really starting to get on my tits. I've told you, soon as we get the readies, you'll be out of here.'

Chapter 10

'Where are we going, again?' Marlowe asked Jenny as he eased the Mondeo out of the station car park.

'Sidmouth Street, 15b, a first floor flat.' Jenny said as she settled herself in the passenger seat.

'Can't understand it, a perfectly good home in Cottingham, right on the university's doorstep and he chooses to live in a crappy bedsit,' Marlowe said as he drove the Mondeo down the Boulevard towards Anlaby Road.

'Wants his independence I suppose, cut the apron strings. Didn't you want your independence when you were his age boss?'

'Oh, I got mine alright, my old man threw me out,' he didn't elaborate any further. 'C'mon, move over,' he yelled at a white transit van.

'Sure, you're ok boss, you seem a bit het up?'

'It's just this business with the lad, brings back some painful memories.'

Jenny didn't know whether he was referring to his ex-wife or the fact he'd been forced to leave home and she wasn't going to ask.

'Yeah, well....' She left the sentence hanging. 'Take a left here,' Jenny said as they approached Sidmouth Street.

'Which one is it? I bet you a quid it's the one with the National Front poster in the front window,' Marlowe said as he pulled the Mondeo into the kerb edge.

'Ever the cynic.'

'You mean "ever the cynic", sir.'

It wasn't.

'If you say so, boss. Either way you owe me a quid!'

Marlowe smiled at the cheek of it.

Standing on the pavement outside of 15b Marlowe asked. 'You *do* have a key?' Jenny gave the DCI a "do I look stupid" kind of look. 'I'll take that as a yes,' Marlowe tried the door handle, the door wasn't locked. 'Very trusting around here, come on.' The grimy white plastic double glazed front door of the shared student house opened into a narrow hallway. 'Don't forget to wipe your feet... on the way out,' Marlowe said as he looked down at the filthy hall carpet. The wooden panelled door to Rab's flat faced them at the top of the stairs. The narrow staircase creaked with every step. Marlowe put the key into the lock of the door facing them.

'Before we go any further, boss.' Jenny passed him a pair of Nitrile gloves.

'Thank you, Sergeant.' He pulled on the tight rubber gloves. 'Might stop us catching something contagious,' he said as he turned the key and unlocked the door. Marlowe eased the door open with the toe of his shoe. 'Bloody hell, I wasn't expecting this, I thought it would be a shit hole full of beer cans and fag ends,' he said as pushed the door wide.

'Tidier than my flat,' Jenny said as she entered and looked around, 'and smarter. You should have seen the dump I had to live in when I was at university.' Jenny had taken a Law Degree at Sheffield Hallam University and joined the police force on the "fast track" programme.

'Yeah, well, that's what money does for you. What you need to do is find yourself a rich sugar daddy.'

'You offering, boss?' she joked.

'Believe me, Jenny, there's no way I could keep you in the manner to which you've become accustomed,' he replied light heartedly.

It may have been called a bedsit, but Charles Bacuss's money had paid for what could only be described as the ideal bachelor pad. Both officers stood amazed, solid hardwood flooring, designer furniture and a state of the art flat screen plasma television in the pride of place fixed on the wall. 'So much for wanting to live like a "real" student,' Marlowe said. 'Have a look in the bedroom.'

Jenny disappeared into the bedroom while the DCI checked over the living room. Everything seemed to have a home, nothing appeared as if it shouldn't be there.

'This is borderline OCD,' she called from the bedroom.

The main living area looked to be in the region of twenty square feet with a galley style kitchen at one end, no need to use the communal kitchen with the other occupants of the house. There was a good collection of crime fiction paperbacks and study books on various subjects, on the shelves fixed to the wall below the television. Marlowe flicked through a few books, as expected, there was nothing hidden between the pages. On the coffee table Rab's laptop rested amongst a pile of mountain biking magazines. Along with a pack of cards and some poker chips. 'Seems the lad likes to gamble a little,' Marlowe said as Jenny came out of the bedroom. 'Anything?' he asked.

'Just the usual, nothing that I wouldn't have expected, bugger all looks out of place or looking iffy. Even the bed was made up.'

'Porno mags?' he asked.

'As I said, the stuff you'd expect to find in a single blokes bedroom.' Marlowe gave her an upraised eyebrow. 'Not yours of course, boss.'

'Have a quick look in the bathroom and then we'll get the Crime Scene Examiners or whatever they're called this week to come and do their stuff. You never know they might come up with something useful.'

A quick search of the bathroom produced nothing, it was like the rest of the apartment, spotless. Nothing that could help the investigation. 'When we get back check and see if Bacuss senior supplied the lad with a cleaner, I can't see young Jack- the- lad living in a place this tidy without any help.' Marlowe stood in the centre of the living room. 'Haven't got a screwdriver in that bag of yours have you?' he asked Jenny seriously.

'Screwdriver, why?' She asked, puzzled.

'Wouldn't mind that telly. Think they'd notice if I borrowed it?' Jenny shook her head in dismay. 'Okay, grab the laptop, might find something useful on it. Let's lock up and get back to the nick,' the DCI had a quick last look around.

Jenny's mobile rang just as they were settling into the car. 'Sarge, it's Tanya - Bacuss senior received an MMS from the abductors about five minutes ago.'

'And?'

Jenny put the phone on loud speaker. 'It was a photograph of the lad with a bloodied face, holding up a copy of this morning's *Sun*.'

'Was there text to go with it?'

'"Won't be long now, stay by your phone." I'm sending it to your phone now.''

'Is that it?' The DCI shouted at the mobile.

'Yeah, that's it.'

'The monitoring of their calls, has it been set-up yet?'

'Takes time, boss, KCOM's reckon we should have access to the landline by lunch time. Their mobile provider says anytime now.' The city of Hull has always been proud to boast of having its own independent telephone system.

'Right we're on our way back, Tanya. In the meantime, tell Jonno to grab a hold of Lee and get to the university and start making some enquiries in the admin department. You fit?' he asked Jenny and pulled the Mondeo away from the kerb without waiting for a reply.

Back at the nick Tanya hung up the phone. 'Jonno, you busy?' she called across the squad room.

DC Johnny Lawson, aka "Jonno" was the oldest member of the squad and was well respected by DCI Marlowe, they went back a long way. Jonno had never craved promotion, he liked the solid police work and couldn't be arsed with the stress and political misgivings that came with promotion.

'And why do you want to know?'

'The PI wants to further your education.'

'Stop pissing about, Tanya, what does he want?'

'Okay, don't get snappy. The PI wants you down at the University to see what you can find out about the Bacuss lad. He said to take Lee with you.'

'Why didn't you say so?' Jonno stood up, put his reading glasses in a desk drawer and grabbed his coat from the back of his chair. 'Well, what are you waiting for?' He said to Lee who had his head stuck in the *Daily Sun*.

Lee tut tutted and shut the paper, stood up and grabbed his own jacket from the coat stand and put on.

'Did you go to Uni, Jonno?' Lee asked as they walked out of the nick towards the designated CID pool car.

'Don't be bleedin' daft, University of Life me, ordinary people didn't do things like that in my day. It was only posh grammar school lads who went to University.' Jonno clicked the key fob. 'This is us,' he said, heading towards a dark blue Ford Focus. 'What about you?' he asked once he was settled into the driving seat.

'Could have done, got a place at Leeds to study law, but didn't bother, applied to the force and was lucky enough to get selected. It's harder now to get in than it was in your day.'

'If you say so, Lee.'

Jonno drove the three miles to the University, the car park was full. He pulled up on double yellow lines next to the sports field and put a sticker on the windscreen. "Police". The University of Hull's main campus was situated along Cottingham Road, towards the north of the city, a vast complex of traditional "red-brick" and modern educational buildings.

'What's this lad studying?' Jonno asked as they walked across the car park to the main buildings.

'Media Studies, apparently.'

'And what's that all about?' Jonno asked.

'Three years of skiving, that's what it is mate.' They both laughed.

'Which building do we want?'

'Buggered if I know, may as well stick our heads here and ask someone with an education,' he nodded his head towards Costa Coffee.

'Good idea, I'll have an Americano.'

Twenty minutes later they'd finished their coffee and Lee came away with the mobile number of a young woman he'd been chatting with.

'Never miss a chance do you?' Jonno said as they walked out of Costa's.

'Never,' Lee waved over his shoulder as they headed for the Media Studies Department.

The detectives were misdirected several times along the corridors of higher education. Eventually they found their destination, very near to where they first started. Jonno knocked on the door and walked into the Media Studies administration department.

'Yes, can I help you?' The middle aged, frosty faced gate keeper with a purple rinse hairdo asked, barely looking up from her computer monitor.

'I'm Detective Constable Lawson and this is my colleague DC Kristianson,' said Jonno as they held out their identification.

'How can I help you?' asked Frosty.

'We're making enquiries regarding a student registered in this department, Robert Bacuss?'

'Drugs I suppose. I'm not surprised, they're all at it.'

'No, not drugs, Mr Bacuss has gone missing and we're speaking with anyone who knew him,' Lee said firmly, only to receive one of "those" glances.

'I'm sorry I can't help you.'

'Surely you have contact with the stud...' Lee was abruptly cut off mid-sentence.

'Officers, do you know how many students I have to deal with?' She looked into their blank faces. 'No, I didn't think so, I keep my distance and just get on with my job.'

Jonno was getting to end of his patience. 'Mrs... I never caught your name?'

'It's Ms - Ms Baker.'

'Ms Baker,' emphasising on the Ms. 'This is a very serious situation, Robert may be in danger and we need to speak to anyone that knows him.'

'If it's that serious I suppose you could always have a word with his tutor, Dr David Brown.'

'And where will we find him?'

'Room fifteen, left out of the office, down the corridor and around the corner.'

'Thank you, you've been very helpful,' Jonno said sarcastically. The comment was wasted; she just put her head down and carried on with her *important* work.

'What a cow-bag,' said Jonno once they were back in the corridor. 'That's why she's still a Ms, no bugger will marry her.'

'Cantankerous, just like my Nan,' Lee said, as he led the way down the institutional magnolia painted corridor.

'This is us, room 15,' said Jonno.

Lee knocked on the door. 'Hope this bloke's more helpful than that old bag.'

'Come.' A voice on the other side ordered them to enter.

'Another arse by the sound of it,' Jonno said as he pushed open the door.

The room was large, in the region of fifteen feet by twenty feet, the walls lined with bookcases. Two battered armchairs were set out before a mahogany veneered desk that was piled high with books and papers. Behind the desk sat a youngish man with spiked hair, black rimmed spectacles and sporting a week's growth of beard.

'Mr Brown?' asked Jonno.

'Dr Brown,' he corrected, 'and you are?' he asked, remaining sitting.

Once more Jonno made the introductions.

'Please, take a seat. What can I do for you gentlemen?' He reached over the cluttered desk to shake hands.

'We're making enquiries about one of your students - Robert Bacuss.'

'Not in any kind of trouble I hope?'

'It depends on how you define trouble. The lads gone missing and we're trying to trace his whereabouts. So, anything you can tell us about him may help our investigation.'

Lee sat on the edge of his chair and took out his notebook ready.

'What can I tell you? He's a bright lad, as they say he could do better if he applied himself, he's on course for getting a second class degree. Maybe even getting a first if he put his mind to it.'

'Have you had any problems with him at all?'

'None whatsoever, never misses his tutorials and I believe he has a good record for attending classes and lectures. Can I get you any drinks at all?'

'No thanks, we're fine. Do you know any of his friends?'

'Not really, no, I do know he's friendly with Michael - Mick Harrison, they usually turn up for tutorials together. That's all I can tell you really. The girls in the office can let you have Harrison's address.'

'We've already had a word with Ms Baker.'

'Ah,' he said almost apologetically.

'Thanks for the help Dr Brown, if you think of anything that might help,' Jonno passed across one of his business cards.

'No problem, anything you need just give me a call on extension 221.'

They stood, shook hands with the young educator and left.

'He looked young to be a Doctor,' Lee said, as they walked back towards the admin department to attempt to glean something useful out of Frosty Face.

'Well, just goes to show what you can achieve if you work hard. Get your head down and do some brown nosing; I reckon you could be a DCI in a couple of years.'

'Yeah, right. Who's going to ask the cow-bag for Harrison's address?' Before he had a chance to protest Jonno shoved him through the open door to her office. 'Thanks for that that mate,' he said when they were once again back in the corridor.

'No problem. Where does the lad live?'

Lee checked out the piece of paper the gatekeeper had given him. 'Just off Newland Avenue.'

'That's handy, it's on our way back to the nick, let's go and have a word.'

Newland Avenue was usually only a matter of few minutes' drive away from the university. Unfortunately for them, they hit the Avenues area across the lunchtime rush. Harrison lived in shared student accommodation at number twenty Arlington Street, midway between Cottingham Road and Prince's Avenue.

'Bet you a quid he's sat watching telly,' said Lee.

'Ah, but what programme?'

'Loose Women?'

'You seem to know a lot about daytime telly?'

'Piss off.' Lee reversed the pool car into a space between a skip lorry and rust coloured Citroen. 'That's all I need,' said Lee as he stepped onto the pavement.

'What?'

'Dog shit,' he replied as he hopped about scraping his shoe along the edge of the kerb.

'You'd better get that off before we get back in the car or you'll be walking back to the nick!'

'That'll have to do,' said Lee as he gave his shoe a final wipe on a tuft of grass growing through the paving slabs.

Jonno stood beside the car looking down the length of the street. 'Brings back some memories does this.'

'How come?'

'I was brought up in this neck of the woods,' said Jonno as they approached the front door of number fifteen. 'Used to think what a load of tossers they were.'

'Tossers, who?' Lee was stumped.

'Students, in those days they were all Hooray Henry and Henriettas with long scarves, calling every one Darling.'

'Bloody dinosaur!' Lee said with a laugh, as he banged on the door with his fist.

He noticed a curtain twitch in an upstairs window, next they heard the thunder of feet bounding down the stairs. The front door was opened by a young man wearing a Hull FC rugby shirt and camouflaged combat pants. 'Who you looking for?' Jonno held up his warrant card and made the introductions. 'Yeah, guessed that bit already. Like I said who you looking for?'

'We'd like a word with Michael Harrison?' said Lee, already taking a dislike to the young man with spiky hair and a bum-fluff beard.

'I'm Mick Harrison.'

'Then we'd like a word with you, can we come in.' Jonno asked politely.

'I'm a bit busy right now...'

'Mr Harrison, you either talk to us now, or in an interview room back at the nick. Now are you still too busy?' Harrison was already getting right up Lee's nose.

'Yeah, ok, what's it about?'

Here we go again thought Lee. 'Out here on the doorstep for everyone to hear what the police are questioning you about?' Lee said in a deliberately loud voice, almost shouting.

'Alright, keep your voice down, *officer*,' he said sarcastically.

Jonno and Lee followed Harrison into the house, closing the door behind them. 'Upstairs,' he said, 'my room's at the front.' He bounded up the threadbare stair carpet.

Lee and Jonno followed. As soon as they walked into the grotty room they knew why Harrison wanted to keep them on the door step.

'Open that bloody window, or we'll all be off our heads,' said Jonno.

The fumes from whatever dope he'd been smoking hung in the air like a fog. Harrison didn't argue, he walked over and opened the window.

Lee thought at least the fumes covered the smell of the dog shit.

'You gonna do me for it or what?' referring to his unorthodox smoking habit.

'Not this time. Can we sit down?' Jonno asked as he took the spliff from the ashtray, stubbing it out and grinding it up.

'Whatever - you going to tell me what it is you want?'

Jonno sat on the edge of the un-made bed while Lee pulled out a hard backed chair and sat and took out his notebook at the ready.

'You're a friend of Robert Bacuss?' asked Jonno.

'Rab, yeah, we're on the same course, what about him?'

'He's gone missing, when was the last time you saw him?'

'Ooh, that must have been Saturday night in the Union Bar,' he lied.

'And you haven't seen him since?'

'Nope, he didn't show his face at lectures this week, thought he must be taking some time out.'

'Never thought to give him a call or text?'

'Never crossed my mind, I'm his mate not his mam.'

'How long have you known him?' Lee asked, looking up from his notebook.

'Two years, since the course started.'

'You're sure that was the last time you saw or spoke to him?'

'Said so, didn't I. Look, you gonna be long? Got things to do.'

'Not much longer, can you give us a list of his friends?'

Harrison took three steps across the room to his rickety desk, dropped into the wheeled typist chair and started scribbling on a piece of paper. Jonno looked to Lee and shook his head. Harrison spun around on the chair and passed over the list.

'That's it?' asked Jonno. There were half a dozen names on the list.

Noncommittal, Harrison shrugged his shoulder.

'These names on the list, are they all at the university?'

'Yep.'

'Thank you, Mr Harrison you've been... very helpful.' Lee took out a business card and handed it over to Harrison. 'If you should think of anything that may help, please give us a call.'

Harrison took the offered card and threw it onto his desk cum table. Then walked over and opened the door, ushering them out as quick as he could, firmly closed it behind them.

'What a tosser,' said Lee when they were back in the street.

'Waste of space that lad.'

'I think we'll make a few more enquiries about Mr Harrison when we get back to the nick, there's just something about him.'

Chapter 11

He pulled the net curtain to one side and glanced down into the street. Jonno and Lee were driving away. Harrison took out his mobile and dialled.

'Paul... it's me, I've just had the coppers around asking about Rab... course I didn't... I said fuck all. I reckon we should meet... okay, see you in the *White Swan* in an hour.' Mick went to the ashtray and tutted when he saw the crumpled spliff. He took out his tobacco tin and skinned up, adding a little something to help him think. The room was once again filled with a dopey fog, he didn't want to waste it and closed the window.

Before the meeting with Mick in the *White Swan*, Paul had to pay a visit to see their young *guest*. Rab was dirty and frightened, he'd lost track of time, he didn't know if he'd been locked away for days or weeks. He heard the locks being opened, stood up from the bed and waited; he knew he wouldn't stand a chance if he tried to make a break for it past the big man.

'Things are starting to move on, lad,' Paul said as he entered the soundproof room. 'Hungry? Rab nodded and Paul placed a carrier bag containing pre-packed sandwiches, crisps and a couple of cans of cola on the bed. Enough to keep him going for a couple of days. Rab sat back down and tipped the carrier bag out beside him and immediately set about trying to open the plastic sandwich wrapper with his teeth.

'Tell me Rab, how much do you think you're worth to your old man? Seven... eight grand... ten?'

'You told me you only wanted what I owe you, seven grand.'

'Yeah, well, I got to thinking, maybe your old man will pay a bit more than that to get you back. I think we'll go with twenty.'

'Get real, Paul, he doesn't have that sort of money.'

'Are you having a laugh, Rab? He owns the biggest carpet retail business in East Yorkshire! You just enjoy your grub while I get sorted.'

Paul picked up a piece of card that had lain on the floor a long time, took a marker pen from his pocket wrote "£20,000 if you want him back" and put it down on the table while he switched SIM cards in the pay-as-you-go mobile.

'Hold this,' Rab had the right idea and held the card in front of his chest. 'Yeah, that's right, good.' he said Then wham, Paul's fist connected with Rab's nose, blood ran freely down Rab and the board. He collapsed backward on the bed sobbing, his nose still not healed from the first assault and was now well and truly fucked. 'Don't start blubbering like a girl, that was just to get the perfect image. Now sit up and hold the card up. Smile!' With the phone's camera Paul photographed Rab holding the card, blood and tears running down his face. 'Nice, that should do the trick, makes the heart strings twinge.' He put the mobile in his pocket, picked up an already bloodied rag and gave it to Rab.

Once more Rab was left alone.

The White Swan public house belonged to a friend of Pauls, it was a drab looking pub situated midway along Beverley Road, next to the old derelict cinema which had been bombed out during the Second World War, the façade stood as a constant reminder. There had been talk of the council buying the place and turn it into a permanent war memorial and education centre. The *White Swan* itself was in just as much a sorry state, to the casual passer-by the place gave off the misconception it was itself derelict.

The interior wasn't much better, drab and miserable, the ceiling yellowed with years of drifting nicotine. The place was desperately in need of a makeover that was never going to come, at least not until the brewery sold the place.

Negotiations with a national chain of theme pubs was already underway.

Mick Harrison was already waiting in the *Swan*, sat at a corner table with two pints in front of him. Paul walked in and looked around. Harrison waved an arm as he saw Paul, not that there was any need, there were only two other customers in the place, both over sixty five.

Paul walked across and sat down. 'Cheers,' he picked up the pint and took a swallow. 'I was ready for that,' he said as he took out his mobile. 'Who's the old bird behind the bar?' he asked as he looked around.

'No idea,' he replied, showing no interest whatsoever.

Paul put his hand in his jeans pocket and took out the mobile. 'Sending this to his old man, what do you reckon?' He showed the picture of a decrepit looking Rab holding the piece of card.

'For fuck's sake, Paul, what's got into you? This has gone beyond a joke,' he passed the phone back. 'I thought it would be all over and done with by now.'

Paul shrugged at the comment. 'What did the police want?'

'What do you think? "When did I last see him, who his friends are", that kind of stuff. Put the wind up me though all the same.'

He picked up the glass and sipped.

'Did it sound as if they had anything?'

'Not to me - no, but then again, I'm not a copper.'

'Well, it won't be much longer then it'll be over. We're gonna tap his old man for twenty grand.'

'You're having a laugh? Twenty grand, that's crazy. Thought we was asking for seven, get the cash quick like?'

'Thought we should go the full hog, not as if his old man can't afford it.'

'Yeah, but, Paul, twenty?'

'I want my pub back up and running. Eddie reckons there's another option.'

'And what's that?'

'Eddie wants to sell him,' he picked up his pint.

'Oh no - no sodding way did I sign on for that.' He stood up to leave.

'Calm down, sit yourself fucking down, Mick. I said to Eddie, "what we gonna do, put him on eBay or sommat?"

but seriously, he reckons he knows a bloke who'd give us a few grand, no questions asked.'

'We're not though are we?' He had a desperate edge to his voice, after all he only wanted to teach Rab a lesson.

'Not if I have my way, he's gonna make us a shed load of money. More than enough to get my pub back.' Paul started playing about with the mobile and pressed a few keys.

'Gone.' The photograph was on its way.

Chapter 12

'Jenny, did you get CSIs to go around to the lads place?' Marlowe asked as she walked past his open door.

'Karina has a team down there now,' she said as she stuck her head around the doorframe.

Karina Taylor was the Senior Crime Scene Examiner, Marlowe thought her to be at the top of her game, if anyone could come up with something useful it would be her and her team.

'To be honest, I think it'll be a waste of time, everything looked in order. What about the laptop?' asked the DCI.

'Lee's a bit of a whizz when it comes to that sort of stuff, so I've let him have a quick look before we hand it over to Hi-Tech Support. You know what they're like, once they get their hands on it goodness knows when we'll see it again, they're always backed up.'

'Okay, let me know if Lee comes up with anything.' Jenny was just about to return to the squad room. 'Don't run off I need a word on another matter, come in.' Puzzled she did as she was asked. 'Close the door, Jenny, make yourself comfortable.' As the door shut the DCI picked up the desk phone and dialled DI Dave Gowan's mobile.

'Dave, can you come through and bring Tanya with you.'

Jenny had fallen foul of the low sprung sofa before and chose the spare chair. 'What can I do for you, boss?'

'Let's hang on until Tanya and the DI arrive.'

Dave Gowan knocked once on the door and pushed it open for DC Tanya Etherington to squeeze past with a tray of coffees.

'Tanya, you're a mind reader,' said Marlowe as she set down the tray.

'Sorry, Sarge, I never got you one.'

'No matter,' Jenny replied.

'Sit down the pair of you.'

The only seating available was the sofa. Tanya sank undignified into the low leather settee. Dave Gowan reluctantly sat beside her with his knees almost touching his chin. 'What can we do for you, boss?' asked Gowan as he nursed his mug of coffee.

Marlowe sat forward in his chair, resting his elbows on the desk.

'It's a bit of a delicate one,' The atmosphere was tense. 'What I am going to say isn't to leave this office, we keep it between the four of us - right?' He looked from one to the other, they nodded. 'The last major inquiry, the one involving Sean Keane, remember we had that pack of Heroin go missing from the safe in the evidence locker.' Sean Keane was a vicious and callous piece of scum who had worked for his Uncle Patrick who wasn't any better.

'Yeah, it turned up in Keane's uncle's safe.' She could hardly forget the case, her friend and colleague DC Lee Kristianson was abducted and almost strung up from a beam in Keane's uncle's stable.

'At least we got it back before the audit people knew it was missing,' Gowan added.

'That's as maybe, but how the hell did it find its way there, that's what I want to know?' He waited a few seconds for a response that never came. 'The top and bottom of this is - I want you to look into it, Tanya, specifically.'

This was a big moment for Tanya, she hoped the pride wasn't showing in her face. Tanya had begun her police career in the East Yorkshire market town of Driffield. Once qualified for a CID appointment, she transferred to Hull, the "Big City" looking for excitement and she found it - of sorts. Maybe not quite what she had expected, but cases she could immerse herself in and occasionally dangerous, as her colleague and friend DC Lee Kristianson could vouch.

'I appreciate where you're coming from, boss, but surely its water under the bridge now?' Dave Gowan said. They had enough on their plate, never mind taking on a semi-cold case.

'Exactly, that's just what whoever took it will be thinking, they'll be off guard. Well, it's far from bloody over. The stuff went missing from a bloody police station for God's sake.'

'If you're feeling so adamant to get to the bottom of it, shouldn't you be passing it on to Professional Standards?' Gowan tried to stick to his guns and not commit.

'That's the problem, Dave, it was me that cocked up by wanting to keep it in house in the first place, when I really should have reported it at the time, but to save myself looking like a pratt I kept quiet.

'That's why I want Tanya on it. Just keep it between the four of us, see where it leads us. Before you go telling me how busy you all are, Tanya can do the leg work with Jenny keeping an eye on this, that'll leave you free to manage things. If you need anything, just ask and I'll see what I can do.'

Gowan knew there was no way out. 'Where to start that's the problem?'

'We may have to revisit the case from the beginning,' Jenny looked to the DCI as she tried to move to a more dignified position on the sofa.

'If you have to, so be it, just keep it discrete that's all I ask.' Marlowe opened a desk drawer and took out a manila folder, sliding it across the desk. 'You might find what we're looking for in there, but for the life of me, I'm buggered if I can.'

Marlowe did what he usually did to signify the end a meeting, he picked up his reading glasses, put them on and started to study another file on the desk.

End of the meeting and they filed out.

'You're going to have your work cut out, Tanya, you do realise there's still the run of the mill jobs that'll need doing.'

'Of course, sir.' She wasn't going to be put off.

'That's it then, Jenny, if you and super sleuth come up with anything I'd appreciate it if you'd run it past me before going to see the, boss?'

'Will do - no probs.' The DS looked to Tanya then stuck her tongue out childishly behind the DI's back. 'Take no notice, Tanya, he's arsey because he's just signed his divorce papers. Like the DI said, any problems just shout out, okay?'

'Thanks, Sarge, I'll go and have a look through this,' she said holding up the file.

Lee Kristianson sat at his desk carrying out a PNC check into Mick Harrison, he was convinced there was something more to Harrison than just being an arrogant twat, he would bet a pound to a penny he would have a record. Lee was disappointed, it appeared as if he was just an arrogant twat after all, the Police National Computer check didn't bring up anything significant. Harrison definitely had an interesting family and some dubious contacts, but nothing other than a minor juvenile record for shoplifting.

Kristianson sat back in his chair and folded his arms around the back of his head and stared at the screen. Then his desk phone rang.

'DC Kristianson.... Ah, Mr Bacuss,' Lee said into the handset. Just the call he wanted - not.

'Have you checked the incoming messages to my mobile?' asked Bacuss with some urgency.

'No, not in the last fifteen minutes. Has something happened?'

'Have a bloody look and you tell me,' he snapped

Lee could hear Bacuss breathing heavily down the phone as he tapped a sequence of keys on his keypad, Bacuss's call log appeared on the screen, just as DI Gowan came into the squad room. 'Bacuss', he mouthed to Gowan. Dave Gowan came over and watched as the picture appeared. 'Oh shit,' he murmured under his breath.

The DI took the phone handset from Lee.

'Mr Bacuss, we're looking at the picture now...'

The picture showed a bruised and battered Rab, holding a piece of card demanding twenty thousand pounds for his release.

'Never mind looking at it, what are you doing about *it*? I want my lad back.' Bacuss yelled, cutting the DI off.

Gowan could well understand Bacuss's frustration, his son had been kidnapped and as far he was concerned the police were doing bugger all to find him.

'I can assure you, Mr Bacuss, we're doing all we can to locate your son, we're moving as fast as we can.'

'Well, it's not bloody fast enough.'

Gowan rolled his eyes. 'I'll ring you back shortly.'

'No you won't - get Phil to ring me with an update.'

'DCI Marlowe's tied up in a meeting just now,' lied Gowan. 'As soon as he's free I'll get him to call you back. In the meantime, I can assure you as soon as we have more information you'll be the first to know. We'll speak soon, Mr Bacuss.' The DI hung up the call before Bacuss's had the chance to yell profanities down the phone. 'Lee, print me a copy of the picture.'

Kristianson pressed the print key and walked over to the laser printer and retrieved the copy.

Lee shook his head as he passed over the picture. 'Jesus, he looks a bloody mess,' said Gowan as he held up the photograph. 'Get onto Bacuss's mobile provider and see if they can triangulate where the message was sent from.'

'Will do,' said Lee picking up the phone and dialling.

'I'll be in with the boss if anybody wants me.'

Gowan knocked on the door once and walked in. 'You'll want to see this, Phil,' he said as he slipped the photograph in front of him. Gowan only ever used the DCIs Christian name when in private.

'What is... bloody hell, Dave, I wasn't expecting that. Doesn't look good does he?'

'Bacuss is demanding you ring him back,' he said as he sat down. 'The embarrassing thing is that Bacuss got the message before we did.'

'How come?'

'No idea, we should have received it the same time he did, then again, maybe we did - we don't have someone sat there 24/7 waiting for his calls to come in. Lee's trying to see where the message was sent from as we speak. You can guarantee it'll have been sent from a non registered pay-as-you-go.'

'I don't know what to make of the demand for twenty grand?' He rocked back and forward in his chair. 'I know it's a lot of money, but I'd have thought that if it was a professional crew, they'd have asked for even more.'

'True, some chancer who reckons he or she can screw a few bob out of Bacuss without too much bother. That's if he has got twenty grand?'

'No need to worry on that score, Dave, if push came to shove, I reckon he could come up with a damn lot more.' Marlowe picked up the photograph once more. Robert was obviously in the sitting position, the backdrop just an off-white colour. 'Not much in the background to give any clues.'

'I'll get High Tech on it anyway. What about Bacuss?'

'I'll give him a call when we've got something to tell him. Did we get a Family Liaison Officer sorted?'

'A uniform from Priory Road,' Gowan took out his notebook and checked. 'Sue Brocklebank, don't know her, but she came recommended.'

Marlowe nodded. 'How did Jonno and Lee get on at the University?'

'Looks like a waste of time, didn't find out anything we didn't know. Saying that, Rab's mates with a lad named Mick Harrison, Jonno and Lee weren't very impressed when they went to see him.'

How come?'

'Seems he's a bit of a "pot" smoker with an attitude. Lee's doing a background check. When he's done, I'm having him look into the lad's movements, he might get more out of the University crowd, him being more their age. And Bacuss, you are going to give him a ring?'

'Yes I am - when I'm ready. Have a word with the Family Liaison Officer, see if she can try and calm him down.'

'Any further thoughts of handing the case over to Serious Crime?'

'Again, when I'm ready.' End of conversation.

Marlowe knew there was no way he could put off making that call to Bacuss, he bit the bullet and picked up the phone and dialled.

Gowan left Marlowe to whatever he was doing and went back into the squad room. 'Lee,' Kristianson turned. 'Get your coat on you're going back to the University.'

'But I never went to...' The DI didn't wait for him to finish.

'Really, you do surprise me? Jonno will take over. I want you to check out the lad's movements, we know he was in the Student's Union Bar on Saturday - who was he with, did he go back with anyone? Sunday he was at the parent's house - anyone see him after that?' Lee was still sitting at his desk. 'Well, what are you waiting for?'

'On my way,' he said and jumped up from his chair, grabbed his coat and was out of the office as quick as a flash. Gowan smiled, Lee was a good lad, but needed keeping on his toes. Promoted from the uniform department of the Gordon Street nick around eighteen months previous, so far the young DC had done a reasonable job. That is if you disregard recently getting himself kidnapped, and almost killed by a psycho. He just needed a kick up the arse sometimes.

As soon as Lee left the squad room his desk phone rang. Gowan picked up the call. 'DI Gowan,' he said into the receiver.

'Inspector, it's Alan Bewes in Technical is DC Kristianson there?'

'Sorry, he's just left the office, can I help?' Gowan asked as he dropped into Lee's chair, rummaging in the desk drawer for Lee's stash of sweets.

'I've done a trace on the text message from the Bacuss mobile.'

'Hope you've got some good news.' He popped a custard and rhubarb boiled sweet into his mouth.

'Not any that will help much. The call pinged on two transmitters, I can't give you a definite search area and the nearest location, but what I can give you is an estimated 200 metre radius on Beverley Road.'

'That's a big area, Alan, what's the approximate centre of the area?'

'Difficult, Inspector, as I said with only two definite pings nothing can be certain, we don't have an accurate triangulation, but an educated guess would be somewhere around the Beverley Road - Fountain Road junction. As I've said it could be from any building within two hundred metres.'

'Thanks for that, Alan, if and when we get another call I'll let you know.'

'Why not make it easier, sign it off and we'll monitor all calls to the number?'

'Sounds like a plan. Thanks again.'

Gowan went over to his partitioned area of the squad room, pulled out the chair and sat down. As the authorisation had already been given for monitoring of all the Bacuss's phones it was just a case of Gowan emailing a copy to Bewes in the High Tech. Then he took a Hull street map out of the drawer. Scanning the map of the area just confirmed his thinking, it was such a densely populated area and there was very little chance of narrowing down where the call had been made from. Maybe if the call had been made from a pub? It was a long shot but he made a note in the log to have the nearby pubs checked out.

Over the top of the dividing partition the DI saw Tanya entering with an arm full of folders.

'Are they to do with what I think they are?'

'And there's plenty more.' Tanya put the folders on her desk and followed Gowan to his semi private space.

'How are you getting on?' Gowan asked, keeping his voice low.

'It's a bit public in here, don't you think?' asked Tanya.

'I do think, I'll have a word with the PI and see if he can organise us some space under some pretence or another.'

'It's a bloody minefield,' Tanya said, 'everything in the duty log for the day the drugs went walkabout is missing. To me it looks like a couple of pages have been torn out.'

'Seriously?'

'I'm hardly going to make a joke about that, sir,' she said solemnly.

'Who had access to the locker?'

Tanya opened her A4 notebook. 'Three people that we know about with access that day, Sergeant Trevor Cleeves, PC Dave Willis and PC Tony Smethurst, I've had a run-in with him he can be a right bolshie arse sometimes.

'You reckon on him being in the frame?'

'Like I said, he's a right pain, but I don't think this is his kind of thing. Let's face it, boss, the evidence locker is hardly secure, anyone can walk into the back room no questions asked.'

'Well, it's hardly going to be Trevor. So that leaves Willis.'

'That's where we start to have a bit of a problem, Dave *was* on the duty roster, but he broke his leg and was on sick leave, his name was never taken off the roster. At first glance to all intents and purposes he was down as having access.'

'What about the computer records?

'That's my next job.'

'Ok, let me know if you need anything.'

In due course, Marlowe did ring Bacuss - Shag Pile Charlie, as expected, he was not a happy man.

'Phil, it's been four days now what the hell are you doing to find my lad?'

'Charles, I can assure you we are doing all we can - it's difficult.'

'I don't care how difficult it is, you're the Police for God's sake,' Bacuss protested. 'You've seen the picture...'

'Charles, calm down, we're following every lead. We'll find him, it's just a matter of time,' Marlowe said trying to reassure him.

'Time is something we haven't bleedin got. I'm telling you when they get in touch I'm paying the bastards, I just want him back.'

Marlowe sighed. 'Now hold your horses, it's not a sensible thing to give in to blackmail.'

'Yeah, well, he's not your son and I'm not sensible.' Marlowe almost jumped as he heard the phone being slammed down at the other end.

'Shit,' he said out loud, as he stood up from his desk and walked out of his office, slamming the door behind him and heading for the car park with his smokes.

As usual Trevor Cleeves was already occupying his regular spot in the car park. 'Bloody hell Phil, you've got a face like a slapped arse,' he said as the DCI came out through the custody door.

'Just been on the phone to Shag Pile, gave me a right ear bending,' he replied as he took out a cigarette and placed it between his lips. Cleeves passed over his lighter. 'Cheers.'

'Let's be honest, you can't blame him, anyone would be the same. It's worse for you because you're personally involved.'

'Yeah, well, it wasn't my bloody choice.' He took a deep draw of the cigarette. 'Bloody woman, it always comes back to her.'

'That's hardly fair, Phil, its circumstances.'

'Suppose so, just thought I'd heard the last of that family.'

Marlowe's frame of mind hadn't softened by the time he went back inside, leaving Cleeves rolling another fag. It was obvious he was in a black mood as he entered the squad room.

'Lee back from the university?' he asked Dave Gowan as he walked over to the DI's cubicle.

'Not yet, be fair boss, he's only been gone an hour.'

'I want this thing moving on - fast, that tosser Shag pile reckons he's going to pay the ransom when they get in touch.'

'He can't do that, probably won't see the lad again if he does.'

'I know that, you know that, we all bloody know it, but would he take any bloody notice?'

Marlowe looked over his shoulder. 'Jonno, have you found out anything about the other lad, what's his name - Harrison?'

'He's got a juvenile record as long as your arm, shop lifting, scamming, mugging etc., etc., did six months in a young offenders unit. While he was there he got his head down and did a couple of A-levels, seems to have turned his life around. Saying that he received a warning when he was caught smoking a joint in the university bar. That's it.'

Then, as if on cue Lee came through the door. 'Boss,' he said as he came into the squad room.

'Well, how did you get on?' Marlowe asked. Not quite the welcome Lee was expecting and looked to the DI who rolled his eyes and shook his head toward the young detective.

Lee perched himself on the edge of Jonno's desk and opened his A4 notebook. 'I spent some time showing the lad's photograph around the bar and coffee shop and it appears no one has seen him since Saturday evening.'

'That we know already,' Marlowe snapped.

Dave Gowan shook his head, subliminally, telling Lee to ignore the comment.

'He was seen splashing the cash on Saturday night in the Union bar, he'd had a big win in a poker game the previous evening,' Lee continued.

'How big a win?' asked Gowan.

'No details, big enough from what I can make out.'

'That ties in with him paying his stepmother back the money he borrowed.' Marlowe said thoughtfully. 'Do we know where the game was held?'

Lee glanced down at his notes. '*The Blacksmiths Arms.*'

Jonno swung around in his chair. 'Funny, I thought that place closed down months ago.'

'According to the people I spoke to he was hyper about it, bragging how he had been invited to play again on the Sunday evening. He was telling anyone who would listen how he was going to make a killing 'cos the people he was playing with were a bunch of no-hopers.'

'What about the other lad, Mick Harrison?'

'He was there, encouraging him, telling everyone how good he was. What is interesting he never mentioned it at all when we interviewed him,' Lee said looking towards Jonno.

'Yeah, he kept that one quiet,' added Jonno

'Good work, Lee,' Marlowe's mood had definitely mellowed. 'I think you two had better bring him in and find out what else he forgot to tell us. Right, back to it, I want something positive on my desk by the end of business today.' He went back to his office closing the door behind him.

Chapter 13

For four days Rab had paced his small "cell", he knew every square inch of the place, not that there was much to know – he did know he couldn't get out. His mind was wavering on the edge, he'd totally lost track of all time since his incarceration. It was driving him crazy being cooped up in the soundproof room.

He stood in the centre of the room. 'Let me out you fucking bastards,' he shouted to no avail, he wasn't expecting to be heard but at least he could vent his frustration. Dejected, he dropped down on the grimy bed and wrapped a blanket around his shoulders, there was little he could do but wait for Paul or Eddie to appear with the obligatory bacon sandwich. Sitting with his back against the wall, he picked up one of the porno magazines he'd found stuffed under the mattress and skimmed through the pages - again. Eyes drooping, more with boredom than tiredness Rab lay against the filthy pillow, filthy from his own blood, wishing he had some smokes.

Then he heard the lock click and a heavy bolt slide.

'Still here then?' Paul said mockingly as he entered the room and locked the door behind him.

'Very fucking funny. How much longer are you going to keep me here?' Rab eased himself into a sitting position.

'As soon as your old man coughs up you'll be out of here.'

'Yeah, like fuck I will.'

'Now, now, no need for bad language.'

'Oh yeah, like you'd be sitting here laughing your head off?' Fighting tears he shuffled back resting against the wall.

'Give it a fucking rest, we'll be contacting your old man again, let's just hope he really does want you back.' He threw a plastic carrier bag down next to Rab. 'Crisps, sarnie, chocolate and a couple of cans of pop, when you do get out you can tell your old man, how well we looked after you.' Paul laughed, turned and left the room locking the door.

'You bastard,' he heard Rab yell as the door closed.

Eddie was waiting in the adjacent workshop.

'I think we'd better get a move on, the lad's starting to crack up,' Paul told him. 'Won't be long before he loses the plot.'

'Yeah, well, there's still the other option.'

'Look, we're not going to fucking sell him, we do it my way and there's a chance we stay out of the nick.' He took out his tobacco tin and skinned up. 'Once we get the cash all we have to do is keep our heads down for a bit, a few weeks in the Canaries, somewhere hot.'

'You really think he's going to keep his gob shut? If you do you're fucking dafter than I thought.'

'Oh, give it a bloody rest; you're as bad as him in there. Come on, let's get out of here and work out where we can get his old man to drop the cash off.' Paul switched off the workshop lights and followed Eddie into the quiet side street, slid the heavy wooden door into place and fastened the security lock. 'We're meeting Mick in the *White Swan*.'

'And that's another thing, we don't need that little wanker anymore,' Eddie said aggressively.

'What the hell's up with you, mate, you've been acting like a daft tart since breakfast in *Fat Sam's*?'

'I just don't like it, Paul. To be honest, I wish we'd never listened to Mick in the first place. Just want it over.' He quickened his pace and strode on ahead. 'Sell the fucker and be done with it.' Paul heard him say quietly.

'It'll be over soon, a few quid in our sky rockets *and* I get me pub back,' Paul replied to Eddie's back.

It was more than evident that Eddie was feeling pissed off at the whole situation, he'd only agreed in the first place when he thought they were just fleecing a few grand out of Rab. The kidnap was an afterthought by Paul.

The *White Swan* was far busier than usual for a lunchtime or any other time for that matter. 'What's goin' on?' Paul asked the old bird behind the bar when he'd shouldered his way through.

'It's been like this since I unlocked the door. The Sports bar across the road, they're doing it up and shut down for a week. I'm working my tits off here.' Paul raised his eyebrows, this was the last thing he expected her to say. 'These soft sods think they can watch the football later,' she waved her arms about, 'they don't know the telly hasn't worked for two years. Three pints of lager, is it love?'

'Please.' Juggling three pint glasses, he edged through the punters to a corner table where Eddie and Mick sat waiting.

'What's up with you?' Mick asked Eddie, who sat there not saying a word.

'Oh, don't bother about him, he's seen his arse. Anyway, I reckon it's about time we ended this,' said Paul.

'Halle - fucking - luiah,' Eddie mumbled as he picked up his pint.

'I've been thinking about where we can get Rab's old man to leave the dosh.'

'Well enlighten us, don't keep it to your bleedin self.'

'For Christ's sake, Eddie, will you just chill,' Mick told him.

'Chill, I'll fucking chill you in a minute.'

Mick sat back in his chair and picked up his pint.

'Are we finished arguing?' asked Paul, looking from one to the other. 'Ok,' he picked up his pint and sipped, then looked at Eddie. 'That cousin of yours, the one that works for Royal Mail...'

'Gordon?' Eddie replied, puzzled.

'Yeah him, you think he'd be up for making some easy money?'

'Don't see why not, he's up to his neck in debt.'

'What I've got in mind is this, it's simple really. We get Bacuss to post the money and then we get your cousin to lift it from the sorting office before it's delivered. What could be easier?'

'Sounds easy,' said Eddie. 'But what happens if Gordon gets caught?'

'Who gives a toss?' Mick said, smiling as he sat back in his chair and picked up his glass.

'You're a little shit, you know that?' Eddie snapped back.

Paul thought the same but kept it to himself. 'No chance, as long as he's careful, it'll be a piece of piss.'

'That's all well and good but...'

'Here we go again, for God's sake, Eddie, what's wrong with you? Paul demanded to know.

'You know what's wrong with me, I want this done with.'

'And I've told you, we're nearly there just have a bit of patience. Here, get some drinks in.' Paul took a ten pound note from his wallet and handed it over. Eddie snatched the note, stood and then walked across the bar mumbling as he went.

'So, you reckon this'll work?' Mick asked, leaning across the table.

'Don't see why not.'

Mick sat back in his chair. 'This lot will kick off when they realise they can't watch the footy,' he said as he looked around at the punters.

Eddie came back from the bar and placed the full glasses down on the table. 'Sorry about being an arse.' Eddie conceded. 'I'll sound him out.'

'Good man. Cheers - here's to money in the bank,' he said, holding up his glass, 'you got my change?' and they laughed.

'I'm gonna sup up and get off before they do kick off,' said Mick.

'What time is the kick off?' asked Eddie.

'As soon as this bloody lot realise the telly doesn't work!' He finished his pint in two big swallows, burped loudly and wiped his mouth with the back of his hand. 'I'm off, see you later,' he said, leaving Paul and Eddie in the *White Swan.*

As Harrison rounded the corner of Sidmouth Street, he never noticed Lee and Jonno waiting in the un-marked police vehicle,

'Here he comes,' said Jonno looking in the rear view mirror.

'Looks as if he's had a few bevies to me.' Harrison weaved slightly as he walked.

'Or he's been smoking some of that wacky baccy. No hurry, wait until he's unlocking the front door, I don't fancy sprinting down the road after him if he legs it.'

'Sprint? When was the last time you sprinted after anything?'

'Cheeky sod, just keep watching.'

Jonno watched Harrison weave his way down the street, he reached the front door and fished about in his jeans pocket, that was when Lee and Jonno walked up beside him.

'Good afternoon, Mr Harrison,' said Jonno as they approached.

'Now what do you want?'

'No need to be like that, Mr Harrison, we'd like you to come down to the station to answer a few questions.' Lee placed a hand on Harrisons shoulder.

'You arresting me or somatt?' he replied, shrugging Lee's hand away.

'Not at all, we just need to clear some things up, that's all.'

'What if I don't want to come and *clear* things up?'

'If that *was* the case we *would* have to arrest you,' said Jonno as he moved closer to Harrison. 'The choice is yours, you come with us to the station voluntarily or, he also placed a hand on Harrisons shoulder only to be shrugged away. 'What'll it be?'

'Fascists,' he said as he put his keys back in his pocket. 'Well, come on then, let's get this fucking done with I've got things to do,' he grumbled as they escorted him to the car. This was all Harrison needed right now, a tug by the police.

'Mind your head now,' Jonno said sarcastically as he manhandled him into the rear seats.

Back at the station Harrison was escorted to a vacant interview room. 'Sit yourself down,' Jonno gestured to a plastic tubular chair. 'Don't go anywhere, the constable here will keep you company,' he said turning to the burly copper. Constable Dave Stephens moved one of the chairs into the corner of the room and sat down folding his arms across his chest, he glared constantly giving Harrison the evil eye, not that he was trying to intimidate him or anything. Then Jonno left the room switching on the red "occupied" light above the door.

'What you staring at?' He asked PC Stephens, who didn't bother to answer, he just continued to glare. 'Please yourself.' Harrison sat back in his chair and tried to stare Stephens out - Stephens won. 'This is beyond a bleedin joke, how much longer am I going to be sitting here?'

Then the interview room door opened.

Jonno entered the room, Lee close behind was carrying a tray with three cups of vending machine, coffee and set it down on the table. PC Stephens stood up and walked to the door. 'Cheers, Dave,' said Jonno.

'Yeah cheers, Dave, thanks for the conversation - not' The PC smirked and closed the door behind him.

'Help yourself.' Lee pushed the tray toward the centre of the table.

Harrison picked a cardboard cup, sipped and pulled a face at the taste of the stewed liquid. 'What am I doing in here? You said I wasn't under arrest.'

'And you're not...'

'Then I'm off.' Harrison pushed his drink away and started to stand.

'Mr Harrison, do you *want* me to arrest you? Because you're going the right way about it, it doesn't make any difference to me one way or the other. Now please, sit your arse DOWN.'

Harrison knew he was beaten and sat down, rocking back on the chair. 'Can we get on with it - places to go, know what I mean?'

Lee opened his A4 notebook on the table. 'Mr Harrison, we're wondering why you didn't mention Robert Bacuss had a big win at a card game on Friday night?'

'Didn't think it was important.'

'Where was the game held?' Jonno asked.

'I'm not sure, think it was somewhere down Hessle Road.'

'Do you think I fell off a Christmas tree, you're telling me you don't know what pubs you went to?'

'You ever smoked, I mean a proper smoke?' He looked from one officer to the other. 'Na didn't think so, I smoked some seriously good shit Friday night, can't hardly remember fuck all.'

You cocky little sod thought Jonno. 'That's as may be, but when we asked if you knew anything that could help us find him you failed to mention there was another game Sunday night.'

'Didn't know did I - wasn't invited.'

'So, you didn't go with Bacuss to the game on Sunday?'

'Just said - didn't get an invite.'

'Do you have an alcohol or drug problem that we should know about apart from the obvious? Lee asked with a sarcastic edge to his voice.

'Nope, just had a top weekend.'

'Same pub?' Lee asked as he leaned forward, resting his elbows on the table.'

'Same pub?' echoed Harrison.

'Yes did the game take place in the same pub the *Blacksmiths Arms?*' Lee's patience was starting to wear a bit thin.

'Who knows - I bloody don't. I'm telling you I wasn't invited and I wasn't there. Where is this *Blacksmiths Arms* anyway?' He was good, he knew the routine. Jonno looked to Lee, they were wasting their time. 'Anything else I can help you with?'

'No, Mr Harrison, I think that will do for now, you've been very...' Jonno hesitated, he really wanted to say a waste of police time but held it, 'informative.'

'In that case I think I'll be on my way,' he said arrogantly, almost pushing his chair over as he stood up.

Lee snapped his notebook shut. 'I'll show you out,' he said as he hurriedly stood blocking Harrison's path and opened the interview room door to escort him to the station foyer. 'I'm sure we'll be meeting again soon Mr Harrison,' Lee said as a uniformed officer showed him out.

'Maybe, maybe not,' Harrison said with his back to Lee as he stepped into the street.

Jonno was standing by the vending machine when Lee went back through to the CID area. 'Well, that was a waste of time and energy.'

'Yeah, so bleedin cocky, I felt like giving him a slap.' Lee replied as he accepted a fresh cup of brown liquid masquerading as coffee.

Jonno laughed. 'I remember the days when you could do that.'

'For someone who's supposed to have got their life together, he's not making a very good show of it.'

'Fancy a ride out when we've had this?' Jonno asked.

'The *Blacksmiths*? I thought you said the place was closed down?'

'By all accounts so did I, but it keeps cropping up it can't do any harm to take a look.'

Twenty minutes later Jonno drove the pool car into Commerce lane, situated close to the city centre. A hundred metres or so further on he pulled up the car into the kerb outside of the *Blacksmiths Arms* on the junction with Edgar Street. Armstrong had replaced the "For Sale or Let" sign high on the wall. To all intents and purposes, it looked as if its been up there a while. 'Looks shut down to me' Lee said as he climbed out, slamming the car door.

Jonno stood with his hands in his pockets, looking up at the red brick building. 'So it does,' To all extents and purposes the public house was unoccupied. 'When I was a teenager this part of the city was a hub of activity, engineers, foundries, they did work for the fish docks. Before the CD Holmes Engineering company and the other shipbuilding companies shut their doors this place used to be as busy as anywhere in the city, day and night. Now look, it's like a wild west ghost town.'

'Tell you what Jonno, for a pub that's been closed a while the paintwork and windows look pretty clean and sparkly,' Lee said, as he cupped his hands to the sparkling widow and tried to peer inside. Lee moved away from the front and walked around the side of the building and tried the side door handle, then banged with his fist on the clean paintwork - no response. Lee then disappeared down an alley that led to the rear of the pub and tried the yard door - locked. Stretching his arms up as far as he could, he grabbed the top of the wall and heaved himself up. Hanging onto the top bricks he peered over then dropped back down and came back to where Jonno was kneeling down on the pavement, his finger trailing in fresh brick dust below the "For Sale" sign.

'What do you reckon?' He looked up at the sign.

'Looks like it's just been put up or replaced. The back way is locked, but from what I could see over the wall there looks to be a fresh supply of empties.'

'Mmmm, there's definitely something odd going on,' Jonno murmured thoughtfully.

'Think we're wasting our time here.' Lee stood swinging the car keys in his fingers. 'Might as well as get back to the nick.'

Jonno took the car keys from Lee. 'I'll drop you back at the nick. Chase up the Land Registry, find out who actually owns the place and what have you. What else you could do is get the city centre CCTV team to see if they can pick him out on Sunday. If he did go to the *Blackies* he has got to been picked up somewhere.'

'Where are you heading off to?'

'The brewery, see when and why they closed the doors.'

Once he'd left Lee at the nick Jonno headed to the Hull Brewery headquarters, based in the Maltings in the city centre. The Maltings was a mix of refurbished office units and luxury apartments. The Hull Brewery was housed in the central building close to the complex reception area. Jonno pressed the intercom button close to the plate glass door.

'Good afternoon, how can I help?' a woman's voice asked through the external speaker grill.

'DC Lawson, East Yorkshire Police,' Jonno said into the speaker.

'Push the door, please,' the voice said as the door clicked unlocked.

'Hi, how can I help?'

111

Jonno held his warrant card for her to see. 'I'm after some information?'

'May I ask what kind of information?' she asked, squinting through an over long one-side fringe.

'I'm interested in the *Blacksmiths Arms*.'

'The place was closed some months ago, let me see if I can find someone - please take a seat.' She picked up the telephone and dialled. Jonno looked around the reception area, old fashioned solid wood furniture and proper armchairs, black and white photographs of the company's pubs hung tastefully on the walls. Jonno sank back into one of the chairs as she put down the telephone handset. 'Mr Moors will be out in a couple of minutes, can I get you a drink or anything?'

Jonno shook his head. 'No, I'm fine thanks,' and picked up a copy of Public House monthly and scanned the pages. He looked up from the magazine as he heard a door open.

'DC Lawson?' A tall, slim grey haired chap asked as he walked over carrying a folder in his left hand, he held out the other hand. 'I'm Dave Moors, account manager for the Hull area.'

Jonno stood up. 'That's me,' he replied, taking the hand and shaking. 'I'm interested in the *Blacksmiths Arms* on Commercial Lane.'

'So Cindy told me, it's all in here,' he said, placing the folder down on a highly polished occasional table between two armchairs.

'Any information you can let me have would be great,' Jonno sat down again and took out his notebook.

'Well, as you'll probably know the place is closed for business or you wouldn't be here.'

'What I'd like to know is when, why and who ran the place,' Jonno settled back in the chair resting his notebook on the table.

Moor picked up the folder and opened it. 'They'd been having financial difficulties for some time, it started as the larger employers closed their doors. Gradually, as more businesses closed things worsened, consequently we had to take action. We didn't like having to serve notice, the place had been a customer of ours for the past twenty years or so, we used to have a good working relationship with the family.'

'What was the problem?'

'Basically the lack of customers, no customers equal no sales. We did what we could, helped them with promotions etc, but as you know the area has been deprived over the years with the closing down of the local industries. Eventually it got so bad they couldn't pay the outstanding money they owed so we had to take legal proceedings, other creditors followed suit.'

'You keep saying "they"?'

'Figure of speech, it was a family owned pub a "free house", towards the end one of the son's took over the business.'

'And that was - is?'

'Sorry, Paul, Paul Armstrong he took over when his mother decided she'd had enough.'

'So when did they actually lock the doors?'

Moor referred to the folder and flicked over a couple of pages. 'Three months ago, the licensee had no other option other than to put the *Blacksmiths Arms* up for sale.'

'Has there been any interest?' asked Jonno.

'Unfortunately, no, not a glimmer of interest.'

'None of the big chains interested?'

'The location is far from perfect for a family theme pub.'

'Have you an address for Mr Armstrong?'

'I have indeed.' Moors opened the file and took out a loose page. 'Cindy, copy this, will you, please.' Cindy came from around the reception desk, took the paper and headed for the copier. A few minutes later she returned and passed a copy to Jonno.

'Thanks. So he still lives above the pub,' he said as he scanned the front page. 'I appreciate your help and time, Mr Moor. I would appreciate it if you would keep this conversation between ourselves as the investigation is ongoing.'

'No problem,' Moor replied as he stood up and offered his hand.

Chapter 14

Harrison had plenty of time to sober up whilst in the police station. Feeling a little dehydrated his mouth felt like the bottom of the proverbial bird cage. In the newsagents opposite the Gordon Street Station he bought a bottle of water. He opened the bottle and took a swallow, then screwed the cap back tight. Harrison took out his mobile and called Paul as he walked along the Boulevard towards Anlaby Road. 'It's me - we gotta meet.'

'Bit busy just now can't it wait until later?'

'No it fucking can't wait till later,' Harrison challenged down the phone.

'Alright, keep your bleeding hair on, what's the problem?'

'The problem is I've spent the last two hours with the cops.'

Silence.

'Ok, we'll meet you at the yard in half an hour.'

'See you in a bit.'

Mick did an about turn and headed up the Boulevard towards Hessle road. The scrap yard was only a fifteen minute walk away down a narrow side street off English Street, two minutes away from the *Blacksmiths Arms*. The chain on the scrap yard gate hung loose, unlocked. Harrison pushed the heavy metal mesh inwards, as he did a large long haired German Shepherd guard dog ran up barking, dragging its chain behind it.

'Hey Rocky,' Harrison dropped to a crouch and made a fuss of the dog, Rocky sniffing his crotch. It was the same dog that had frightened the life out of Rab as he ran along the alley a few nights previous. The guard dog looked hard, vicicous and mean to the outsider, but to those who knew the dog he was a big soft "pussy cat". Harrison made his way between the piles of dog shit and the heaps of rusting junk over to the portable building that served as the office. He banged on the door with his fist, then walked in, the plywood floor sagged beneath his feet. The place had seen better days but served its purpose. The walls coloured nicotine yellowy brown from years of smoking rollups, on the wall were girlie calendars from years ago all with well worn thumbed corners. Paul sat in an old battered armchair with his feet up on the desk. Eddie was by the kettle brewing up.

'So they dragged you in then?' asked Eddie as he dropped the tea bags in the mugs and filled them with boiling water.

'Yeah, they were waiting for me when I got back home, should a stopped in the pub,' he said as he sat himself on a free standing car seat out of a scrapper.

'Asking questions about young Bacuss?'

'What else?' Harrison reached over and accepted a mug of tea. 'Cheers.'

'You reckon they're on to something?' Paul asked as he squashed the tea bag in his mug and splashed in some milk.

'Maybe - fucked if I know what, but I do know they think there's something a bit iffy going on with the pub.' Paul swung his feet off the desk and sat forward in his chair. 'Kept asking if I knew about a poker game at *Blackies*.'

Eddie walked over, the de-laminated floor bouncing under his weight, he stood in front of the desk and leaned across with his hands palm down on the surface. 'I knew it, we should have fucking sold him when we had the chance. What did you tell em?' he demanded to know.

'Nowt, played dumb didn't I - said I was well out of it and didn't know where we ended up,' he replied confidently as he took out his tobacco pouch and skinned up. 'I'm telling you they've got nowt on me.' He lit his rollie hanging from his lip with a cheap disposable lighter.

Paul sat quiet listening.

Eddie slapped the palms of his hands on the desk. 'It seems to me they've got you sussed, if they know about the poker game and *Blackies* then we've got cause to be worried.' He looked to Paul who raised an eyebrow.

'Take a chill pill, Eddie,' Mick replied cockily with a smile on his face.

'I'll give you a fucking chill pill. How long do you reckon it'll be before they cotton on to us?' He picked up his mug of tea and drank noisily, then banged the mug down spilling the contents on the desk. 'Not fucking long.'

'Come on, Eddie how many times have I got to say it? They've got fuck all on ME.'

'Are you bloody thick or what? You let that little shit Bacuss blab his mouth off about winning at cards to anyone who'd listen. Of course the cops are interested in you – they're not fucking thick.'

Mick stood to his full five feet six and faced the larger man face on. 'And I am?' Mick challenged as he edged even further to Eddie.

Paul banged a fist on the desk. 'Stop behaving like a couple of idiots.'

Mick pointed a finger and poked Eddie in the chest. 'I'm not having this twat speak to me like a kid or sommat,' he turned and walked out of the office.

'Just leave him, he'll get over it,' Paul told him

'I'm not having that little shit, poke and prod at me,' he said following Mick out into the yard. 'Oi, don't walk away from me,' he grabbed Harrison by the shoulder. 'Who the fuck do you think you are? Just because you go to "Uni",' he said in a childish sing song voice, 'you think you're better than the rest of us, that it?'

'Enough, Eddie, just piss off,' he turned to face Eddie trying to shrug the big man's hand away and raised his right arm. Eddie misread the action, let go of Harrisons shoulder, stepped back and with both arms outstretched, he pushed Harrison in the centre of his chest. The younger man was caught completely by surprise and fell backwards into a pile of junk. He lay there not moving for what seemed an age, but in reality was only a few seconds.

Eddie stood over Harrison looking down. 'Get up you little twat, I'm not finished talking to you.' Harrison lay still and quiet, not moving. 'Come on stop fucking about,' he said prodded him with the toe of his work boot. Harrison's head rolled to a side, a dark pool of liquid escaped from around a jagged piece of metal embedded in the back of Harrison's head. Blood mingled with engine oil on the hard mud floor. 'Paul,' he yelled, 'get out here quick.' He dropped down on his knees next to the lad who stared back wide eyed, sighed and then his eyes closed. Eddie frantically felt the side of his neck for a pulse, then put his ear to Harrison's mouth, nothing - the lad was dead.

The door slammed behind Paul as he came into the yard. 'What the... what the fuck have you done to him?' Paul demanded to know when he saw the lad lying on the floor.

'It was an accident, I just shoved him and he went down,' Eddie stood with his hands folded over his head, shuffling from one foot to the other.

Paul dropped to his knees. 'Mick - Mick, come on mate, wake up.' Bent over the lad, he cradled his head as the blood seeped through his fingers. 'What you done, Eddie? Paul repeated. 'Ring for a fucking ambulance.'

'Think it's too late, - what are we going to do?' He paced around and around Harrison's body.

Paul lifted his head, tears ran down his face. He'd known Mick since he was a toddler. He carefully lay Mick's head back on the floor. With a grimy sleeve he wiped the tears from his face. 'He's only a kid... go get a blanket or something from the office. Eddie pulled himself together, ran across the yard and stormed in and desperately looked around, he opened a store cupboard door, reached inside and dashed out again carrying a grimy dust sheet.

'Spread it out,' Paul ordered.

Eddie cleared away the debris on the hard mud and as best he could spread the sheet on the floor. 'It was an accident, Paul, honest.'

'Just give me a fucking hand - easy,' he said as Eddie's meaty hands grabbed the lad's legs. Carefully between them, they lifted Mick Harrison onto the sheet. The two big men lifted him as if he weighed nothing and placed him down again on the sheet.

'I tell you, Paul, it was an accident. I shoved him, that's all, a shove and down he went like a pile of shit. What are we going to do?'

'Don't fucking know do I? Need time to think,' he said as he gently wrapped Mick Harrison in his filthy shroud. With care he lifted Harrison's limp body, tears still running down the biker's face as he carried him into the office and carefully laid him on the moth eaten settee. Paul knew exactly what he was going to do, make sure Harrison was found and taken care of properly. He sighed and dropped heavily into his battered chair. He reached down and opened the bottom drawer of the desk. Took out two glasses and a bottle of Grant's Whisky then poured two generous measures.

'This bloke - the bloke you reckon would buy Bacuss, who is he?' He shoved a glass across to Eddie and picked up his own. The amber liquid burned its way down his throat as he knocked it back in one. He poured another.

'Derek Stephens.'

'You think he'd still be interested?'He knocked back the second and grimaced, then refilled his glass for the third time.

'Only one way to find out, I'll give him a bell and set up a meet.'

'Do that.'

'But what about the ransom?' asked Eddie.

'I think things have gone far enough, I just want it finished with. You just get it sorted, I've got something to do.' He stood up and walked over to the settee tucked the filthy shroud tighter around the body of Mick Harrison.

'What?'

'Tidy this bleedin mess you've got us in.'

'It was an accident - you know that, don't you?'

'Yeah, you've said.' He took down the van keys from a hook in the wall and then stormed out of the office with a tear running down his cheek.

At the other end of the yard in the lockup, Rab sat huddled on the bed wrapped in a filthy blanket. Oblivious to the events that were unfolding he wondered when it was going to be over.

Chapter 15

'Okay, before I go and see the DCI and get my bollocks chewed off, what do we know so far?' DI Dave Gowan asked as he stood in front of the squad room holding an impromptu catch-up. 'Don't all speak at once,' he looked around at the blank faces, 'Jonno start us off.'

'We pulled the lad in again, Michael Harrison...'

'Right little basta...' cut in Lee.

'Okay, Lee, let Jonno finish.'

'Sorry, boss.'

'As I was saying,' he cast a glance towards his young partner, 'to be blunt he was taking the piss, trying to play us for fools and denied everything.'

'If you ask me, I reckon he's got selective amnesia,' Lee added.

Jonno carried on. 'Couldn't remember where the game was played, said he didn't know where the *Blacksmiths* is - absolute bollocks, but until we get something to tie him in we can't prove a thing.'

'And the brewery?' Dave Gowan.

'I spoke with the regional Sales Manager,' he glanced at his notes. 'Dave Moors, he'd had dealings with the *Blacksmiths* for years. Turns out they had some serious money problems, not helped by the fact most of the business's in the area have packed up or moved away.

Seems there was no other option other than put the place up for sale.'

'Who initiated the sale, the brewery?' asked Gowan.

'Indirectly, the place was a "free house", not tied to any particular brewery, but the debts were mounting, they owed the Hull Brewery a fair amount. Paul Armstrong is still registered as the licensee.'

'Got an address for him?'

'Strange that one, he's still on the brewery books as living in the flat above the pub.'

'Then why haven't you brought him in?' The DI questioned.

'When we paid a visit earlier, there was no sign that the place was occupied,' Lee was quick to add.

'But saying that the exterior of the place looked as if it's been tarted up and it looked as if the empties in the back yard hadn't been there long.' Jonno quickly replied.

'Tarted up, in what way?'

'Paint work all washed, windows cleaned that sort of thing, not what you'd expect of a place that'd been closed for business for months.

'According to, Moors, Armstrong has another business, scrap, he's in partnership with,' he checked the notes, 'Eddie Marriot.'

'Where's the scrap yard?'

'All he knows is that it's not far from the *Blackies*, somewhere on English Street.'

'Okay, that's another angle, find the yard. See if all this ties together, Armstrong, Marriot and Harrison. Get uniform to keep an eye on the pub, he's got to show sometime. I'll let the boss know, not that we've got much to report.'

'Will do, I'll try a search on Google.'

'There is something else, before you go take a look at this.' Jonno put a DVD in the player, it was the town centre CCTV for the previous Sunday evening. 'This is just before 7.30pm Sunday night.' A taxi pulled up in Queen Victoria Square outside of the City Hall. 'That's him, see, and keep watching he turns to face the camera in a second.' Robert Bacuss turned as he paid off the cab driver and walked towards the Punch Hotel.

'So he was definitely going somewhere Sunday night. Were there any other sightings?'

'One, twenty five minutes later he comes out with another man...'

'Let me guess, Michael Harrison?'

'Yep, they walk along Carr Lane, then we have a problem - the next camera was out of order but...'

Gowan cut in before he could finish. 'It looks like they were heading in the general direction of the Blacksmiths?

'Oh yes, cos they were picked up again by the traffic cams at the Castle Street roundabout heading down Commercial Road.'

'Then have Harrison brought back in. I'll go and update the boss.'

Eddie was alone in the yard office, alone, except for the body of Mick, who was laid out on a threadbare sofa. 'You had to shout your fucking mouth off didn't you? If you hadn't been so fucking gobby you wouldn't be laid out there would you?' He said to Mick - as if he was listening. It had been a tragic accident, but who would believe him? Not the police, never in a million fucking years he was certain of that. One thing he was certain of, he wasn't going to do time for the clever little shit. He and Paul may have been friends and partners, but he was buggered if he was going to take the blame - if anyone was, it wasn't going to be him.

Eddie knew a thing or two about DNA transference, after all he had been arrested in the past. He put on a pair of Paul's work gloves and loosened the sheet that was wrapped around the body of Harrison. Rubbed a gloved hand over the lad's shoulder, the one he had grabbed. Next Eddie reached up and took a hold of Paul's woolly hat and unhooked it from where it hung on a nail in the wall. He turned the hat inside out and carefully removed a few hairs that were entangled in the wool and tucked them inside the lad's jacket. Holding Mick's hand with the excess sheet material he rubbed the hat into the finger nails of Harrisons hand's. Satisfied that he'd left enough traces of DNA to lead back to Paul, he carefully re-wrapped the sheet tightly around Mick's body and replaced the gloves, as he heard the rough engine of their old transit van being parked up outside the office.

Paul reversed the Ford Transit they used for shifting scrap as close as he could to the office and opened the rear doors of the van wide. Eddie stood and watched as Paul carefully picked up the lightweight body. He followed him to the door and watched as Mick was gently laid in the back of the van. He knew what he had to do, he didn't like it, but there was no other option open to him as soon as it was dark. He was taking Mick Harrison somewhere where he knew he would be found quickly and taken care of with dignity.

Chapter 16

Eddie needed a fag. He was having difficulty in stopping his hands from shaking. They had a life of their own as he tried to flick the wheel on his cheapo lighter. All he had wanted to do was put the little shit in his place, he didn't mean to harm Harrison - just show him he wasn't in charge.

He got up and walked out of the office without a word. He walked with no particular purpose, head down, he just walked, he needed to clear his head. The next thing he knew he found himself on the river front, leaning on the safety barrier he watched the gulls walk in the mud below. What he really did need was a pint, but in the mood he was in one pint would lead to another, and another and it wasn't the time to get pissed. He sat on a wooden bench by the old ferry terminal on Victoria Pier, with his head in his hands staring out over the murky River Humber.

What a fucking mess, he had been in some scrapes in his time, but this - this took the biscuit. He flicked his cigarette butt into the Humber mud. At first it had seemed so easy, nothing could go wrong, a couple of card games and rip young Bacuss off. At the same time pocketing a few quid and that should have been it. But no, Paul had grander ideas. He had his own thoughts on how things should pan out - he was in it for a big payday.

Eddie was the first to admit he also saw pound signs before his eyes when Paul had come up with the idea. But he had another proposal, one which would have produced a quick turn over and get shut of Bacuss. They should have sold Bacuss on. Sold him to someone with fewer scruples than themselves. Someone who didn't mind causing pain and misery, regardless of who they were, and Eddie had known such a person. But no - Paul knew better. Now Paul had done a complete turnaround *he wanted* to sell the lad.

He smoked another fag as he sat staring at the river. 'What the fuck you looking at?' he said to a one legged seagull sitting on the safety rail hoping for a morsel of food. It wasn't his fault that the little shit Mick had a head as soft as egg shell. If only he hadn't let Harrison wind him up, kept his cool with the little shit and ignored him, he wouldn't be sitting here now shitting himself and Mick Harrison would still be alive to annoy him. If only.

The more he thought about it the more he realised they had to sort something and quick, it would only be a matter of hours before the police came sniffing around.

Decision made, hasty, maybe, but he was going to take control - if he could. 'Gordon, it's Eddie,' he said into his mobile. '... Yeah I'm fine, well, sort of, listen did Armstrong get in touch with a proposition?... no, great cos I've got one for you. 'Fancy popping round to my place for a bevy? ... now if you're not doing owt... great see you in a bit,' he hung up.

For the past eight years, Gordon had worked for the Royal Mail as a postman out of the Suttonfields Depot. He had four kids, lived in a council flat and was married to Eddie's sister, a woman who had expensive tastes and most importantly he was always skint. They struggled, it wasn't easy bringing up four kids on a Postman's wage, and Gordon was always on the lookout for ways to make some quick cash.

Eddie himself lived in a council semi along Walker Street not far from the scrap yard. On the way home, he called at the off-licence for some cans.

Thirty minutes later a clapped out old Ford Escort pulled up outside of Eddies. It was Gordon, he was still wearing his Postie's uniform. 'Come in, mate.' Eddie said as he opened the front door. 'Got some cans in the front room.' He looked rough, not only tired from the early morning start but from having to struggle bringing up a young family and expensive wife. Sitting in Eddie's front room with a can of beer in his hand, he confided in Gordon the events of the past days, the card games, the kidnapping and the ransom plans. But - and a big but, he omitted to tell him Mick Harrison lay dead in the back of the van.

'For fuck's sake, Eddie, this is heavy shit You could end up doing some serious time if this goes tits up. How did you let Paul talk you into it? It's a mess, fuck knows how you're gonna get out of this one?' He popped the tab on a can of John Smith's Smooth.

'Yeah, well, Harrison can be a persuasive little shit, I want to run an idea past you.'

'Okay, I'm listening,' Gordon then drank from the can.

'What if we went along with Paul's, original plan?'

'We?'

'Yeah, us.'

'What about, Paul?'

'We cut him out. We do the deal and keep the proceeds to ourselves, no need for Paul to know - think about it?'

'Let me get this straight in me 'ed. You've got this lad stashed in the yard lockup, the lockup owned by you *and* Paul, all of this *was* his idea to start and you want to cut him *out* of the deal altogether.'

'That's the gist of it.'

'You tired of living, got some sort of death wish or sommat?'

'It sounds risky I know, but I reckon inside forty eight hours, Paul will have bigger things on his mind.'

'Like what?'

'You really don't want to know mate, you really don't.'

As the conversation progressed Gordon sat silent, the cogs in his head turning. Then he spoke. 'It'll take more than a bit of organising but I reckon we could do it.' Eddie smiled, he knew Gordon would be up for it. He picked up his can and took a swallow, put the can on the floor and rolled himself a smoke while Gordon gave it some thought. 'When you see these things on the telly, they always get the money dropped off somewhere, and what happens? They alluss get caught.'

'What are you suggesting?' Eddie sat on the edge of his chair, he knew Gordon would think outside the box.

'Why not have the money posted? That way we'll be in control - well, as much as anybody could be.'

'Go on I'm listening.'

130

'First off we'd ave to get the cash sent to a real address, it's got to be a real one with a proper postcode, 'cos if it's not it wouldn't get through sorting - maybe an empty ouse or shop, summat like that,' he took another drink. 'Leave it wi me, I'll find somewhere.'

'And you'd deliver it?'

'Na, we can't let it get that far, 'cos ooever's sending the package will more than likely ave told the coppers and they'll have the place watched. The tricky thing will be identifying the money package, we get hundreds come into the sorting office. If I'm going to nick it. It's got to stand out, be able to spot it quick like.' Gordon swapped his empty can of beer for a full one. 'Maybe get im to send it in a green builders rubble bag, nice and strong and easy for me to spot. Let me think on it, how long have we have got?'

'Not long, forty eight hours max.'

'This tied in with the other thing you've got going with Paul?' Eddie just nodded. 'Ave ya actually demanded the cash from this bloke?'

'Paul told him we'd be in touch soon. But I reckon we've got to move sharpish.'

'In that case I reckon you've got to do this today if you can, give im chance to get the money together. Like you say we gotta be quick like. And another thing, as soon as we get the cash you've got to disappear. When Paul finds out you've stitched him up you'll be dead meat.'

'What about the original idea, setting up an exchange, have him drop the money off somewhere?'

'And ave the cops waiting for us when we collect? No way. I'll ave an address later and you text it to this Bacuss bloke. We don't wanna fuck about on this.'

'I'll have to get the details, Pauls been looking after things so far.'

'Fuck, Paul, just get a hold of the blokes number.'

'Easy, if you can't get his mobile he'll be in the telephone book. If you have to use the landline use a public phone in the city centre or somewhere.'

Eddie liked the way this was going, Gordon actually seemed to know what he was talking about.

'Tell im, this Bacuss, if the parcel's got a tracker in it you'll know.'

'You can tell?'

'Na, but he won't know that. Once I've got the package I'll text you to meet me somewhere on my route and hand it over.'

'How much are we talking about anyway?'

'Twenty thou, split fifty - fifty.' Gordon almost gagged on his beer.

'Fucking hell mate, sweet,' he said and held the can high. 'Cheers.'

Paul sat in the scrap yard office alone, he hadn't heard a thing from his partner since he walked out of the yard. His best guess was that he was holed up in some pub somewhere. 'Well, Mick,' he said, looking through the grimy office window in the van, 'sorry about what happened to you, but you could be a right stubborn bugger when you wanted, and yeah I do reckon it was an accident. I'll take

132

you home, it won't be long before the coppers find you. Sorry, mate.'

It was dark outside, Armstrong checked the time, 1am, well past closing time and the roads would be virtually deserted by now. He put on his leather jacket, checked he had the keys to Mick's flat, locked the office and drove the van with Mick in the back out of the yard, locking the gates behind him. The roads were quiet, a few heavy goods vehicles that thundered along on their way to the docks and the majority of the other vehicles were taxis. Keeping well within the speed limit he drove towards Mick's flat on Arlington Street.

The quiet road was deserted, he had no problems parking right outside of the front door. The biggest obstacle he faced would be carrying the lad up the stairs without disturbing the other occupants of the house. All he would need was some nosey student poking their head around a door to see what was going on. He decided on a two stage operation. He climbed down from the van and closed the door as quietly as he could and locked up. He tried the handle on the front door of the shared house, locked, of course it would be, he thought, after all it was the middle of the bloody night. He took Mick's keys from his pocket. After a quick glance both ways down the street, he put the key in the Yale lock and turned, opening the door as quietly as he could. Armstrong put the lock on the latch and steadily went up the stairs to Mick's bedsit and repeated the operation, leaving the door slightly ajar. He tiptoed back down the stairs, stopped dead and held his breath as he heard movement coming from the door to the left in the hallway - nothing, he speeded up a little.

Leaving the front door slightly open he stepped into the street, it was quiet - no one about, everyone was tucked up in bed where they should be. The sliding side panel door on the Transit made the slightest sound as it was slid open, but to Armstrong it sounded like a Jumbo Jet taking off. Reaching inside, he could easily lift Harrison's wrapped body, rigor was setting in he was stiff. Holding the light weight in one arm, he closed the van door and quickly stepped back inside the house and ran up the stairs, pushed the already open door wide and stepped inside. He kicked the door closed with the heel of his boot. Still with Harrison in his arms, he leaned back against the door and breathed, until that point he didn't realise he had been holding his breath.

Shame he thought as he looked around the bedsit, Mick Harrison had deserved better than this. He lay Mick on the single bed and unwrapped him from the dirty sheet and recovered him with the duvet. 'Sorry it ended like this, Mick,' he said as he left the bedsit leaving the door ajar. Thirty seconds later, after taking the stairs two at a time he was pulling the Transit away from the kerb. It would not be too long before he was found he hoped - he deserved better.

Chapter 17

'So, Lee, you out tonight?' Jonno asked as they drove to *Armstrong - Marriot Motor Dismantlers*. The Google search had come up trumps. Even better was that the yard was minutes away from the *Blacksmiths Arms*, down the appropriately named Mechanics Lane.

'Might pop into the George for a pint when we knock off?' He looked through the side window. 'See the state of that? An old slapper in a mini skirt, and wearing a top that rode half way up her back went past.

'That's the wife,' Jonno replied, trying to keep a serious face. 'Hope she comes back with a few more quid than she did last night,' he said, trying not to smile as Lee turned to face him.

'What?'

'Got to get our holiday money from somewhere,' he didn't crack a smile as he said it. 'This place doesn't look any better than that old tart we just saw,' he said as they pulled up outside the gates of *Armstrong Marriot Motor Dismantlers*. As far as scrap yards went, this was the pits. Old cars piled high, obviously, but these were far from conforming to any health and safety standards anywhere in the world. Lumps of metal and engine blocks filled the spaces between the mounds.

'Right, let's go and have a word in their shell likes,' Jonno said as they left the vehicle.

Then they heard the barking.

'In you go, Lee.'

'You can piss off, you think I'm going in there - sounds like there's a wolf on patrol.'

The barking continued and a heavy set man walked down the yard towards them. He looked the part of a scrapper, grimy one piece boiler suit, steel toe capped boots and a roll-up hanging from his lips.

'Yeah, can I help?' he almost growled in a not so customer friendly voice.

'Police,' Jonno and Lee held the identification to the scrapper. 'We want a word with Mr Armstrong and Mr Marriot.'

'Eddie's out, you'll have to make do with me, I'm Paul Armstrong,' he said as he pulled the gate in towards him.

Jonno was a bit dubious about entering the yard. 'That dog fastened up.'

'Aye, he's on a chain don't worry.'

'But I do worry when they sound like that. He been fed?' he asked, trying make light of the situation.

Armstrong laughed. 'He's a pussycat,' he said as the rattling of the chain grew louder. 'See - told you he was a daft bugger.' A long haired German Shepherd as big as a Shetland pony came bounding up, demanding to be made a fuss of. 'We'll go into the office shall we?' Armstrong turned away and led them through the debris and piles of dog shit. 'Okay, what's this about?' He asked once they were inside the cabin.

He didn't invite them to sit down. Not that they would have amongst the oil and grime.

'I'm DC Lawson and this DC Kristianson.'

'As I said what can I do for you officers?'

Lee took out his notebook. Jonno started off the questioning. 'Mr Armstrong, you were - are the owner of the Blacksmiths Arms, correct?'

'Aye, that's right what about it?'

Jonno watched Armstrong's face closely as he questioned him. He was usually pretty good at spotting a lie.

'Have you opened up the place lately?

'The pub? Jonno nodded. 'Not since we shut the place down. I'm looking for a buyer - you interested?'

Cheeky sod thought Jonno and smiled. 'Unfortunately not. Do you know a young lad called Michael Harrison?'

'As a matter of fact, yes.'

'And how do you know him?' asked Lee, with his head down, making notes.

'I knew his old man before he passed away.' He was trying to stick to the truth as closely as possible.

Lee looked up from his notes. 'Seen him lately?'

'No, just said he passed away.'

'Very funny Mr Armstrong - not.'

'Oh, you mean Mick, not for - let me think, must have been a year or more back before he went off to university. Clever lad, too good for these parts now.'

'Have you come across a friend of Michael's, Robert Bacuss?' Jonno watched closely as he replied.

'Nope, never heard of him.' Oh, he's good thought Jonno.

'What about your partner?'

'What about him?'

'Does he know Michael?'

'Aye, he knows him, but can't speak for him. You going to tell me what this is all about?'

'Just making enquiries, that's all.'

'Well, are you done now? I've got work to do.'

'Just one more question, would you mind if we had a look around the *Blacksmiths?*'

'Yes, I would. Look, I haven't got time for this, come back when you've got a warrant,' he stood up and gestured to the door.

Jonno smiled. 'We might just do that. Thank you for your time, Mr Armstrong,' he didn't offer his hand.

As soon as they were out of the office Paul fished his mobile out of his overall pocket and dialled, the call was picked up by his voicemail. 'Eddie, it's me - the coppers have just been around the yard - fucking call me ASAP.'

'What's your thoughts?' Jonno asked Lee.

'Hard one to read, that's until you asked to look around the pub. Mind that shit,' he said as they picked their way out of the yard.

'Hmm, he definitely gave a twitch or two. The problem is there's no way we can get a warrant to search the pub without firm evidence - and he knows it.'

'That building at the back of the yard, you reckon it belongs to Armstrong and Marriot?' Lee asked as they stood on the pavement looking back into the yard. A single storey brick built building backed onto the scrap yard, no visible door or windows that they could see. They couldn't see Armstrong letting them take a closer look

'Can't see any access from here, might be worth a walk around before we go back to the nick.'

The two detectives walked the cobbled street following the wire fence, they could hear the German Shepherd dragging its chain as it tried to follow their progress. The entrance to the building was on Ropery Street. The access via one large solid timber sliding door that ran on a heavy metal track. The door was secured with a heavy security padlock.

Lee stood back on the road and tried to read the fading hand painted writing. 'Something something Motorcycles, can't make the rest out.'

Jonno gave the lock a tug. 'Been greased up,' he said as he took out his handkerchief and wiped the grease from his hands.

'Same with the track.' Lee looked to Jonno. 'A good place to stash something or someone away.' Jonno gave his usual, "hmm" and banged on the door with his fist a couple of time, he wasn't really expecting any response.

Chapter 18

The DCI was in deep in thought. He supposed he should give Shag Pile a call and let him know what progress they were making with the case - or not. Of course it was important to keep the family informed, but this family - this time he was going to delegate.

DS Jenny Bright knocked on the office door. Marlowe looked up from the computer screen and nodded. Jenny entered.

'Got a problem, Sir.'

'Sounds serious.' It had been a long time since she had called him Sir, she usually settled for Boss.

'Bad news, uniform found the body of...'

Marlowe cut her off mid-sentence. 'Robert?' he flopped back in his chair and put his hands to his head.

'No...'

'Thank heavens for that - that came out wrong, just glad it wasn't Robert'

'I know what you mean. It's the other lad, Mick Harrison. The DI sent uniform to bring him in for further questioning, the door to his flat was already open. He was laid out on the bed. They just radioed to let us know.'

'Shit, from what I've heard he liked his dope, overdosed?'

'Nope, he had a bloody great gaping hole in the back of his head. Uniform has secured the scene until we get someone down there.'

'Okay, get sorted and we'll go and take a look.'

'Shall I organise a car?' She knew what the answer would be.

'No we'll go in my car.' Marlowe much preferred using his old Ford Mondeo for two reasons, it didn't smell foul like most of the pool cars and it didn't have a police radio, much to everyone's annoyance. 'See you in the car-park in five minutes.'

The DCI pushed back in his chair, stood up and reached for his jacket hanging on the chrome coat stand. Put the jacket on and checked the pockets. All okay his cigarettes and lighter were there. His Airwaves radio was in the charging unit on top of the filing cabinet, he picked it up and checked the battery status - flat as a fart, he had forgotten to turn the charger on.

Marlowe was standing by the Mondeo having a quick smoke. Sad that Harrison was dead, but at least he didn't have to go and give more bad news to Shag Pile and Karen. He dropped the cigarette to the floor and ground the butt into the gravel as Jenny walked up.

'Want me to drive?' she asked, only to receive a scowl. 'I'll take that as a no then, boss,' she said as she walked around the passenger side and opened the door.

'Right, Sidmouth Street?' the DCI asked as they buckled up. She nodded.

        He turned the key in the ignition and put the car into gear and pulled out of the station car - park. 'Tell you what, Jenny, I really thought it was going to be Robert's body they found. For a split second I saw myself around at the parent's place explain to Bacuss senior what had gone wrong.'

'Understandable when it's sort of personal.'

Marlowe drove down the Boulevard and under the flyover past the K.C. Stadium then onto Anlaby Road.

'Anything to report on the other business?' Marlowe was referring to the packet of Heroin that had gone missing from the safe in the evidence room.

'I'm struggling, bits of info missing here and there, it's all over the shop. The way it's looking, the only person it could have been is Trevor Cleeves.'

They both laughed out at such a ludicrous suggestion, Marlowe had known Cleeves since they were lads at school.

'Ah well, I'm sure something will turn up, it has to'

The parking situation along Arlington Street was horrendous, a narrow road with double yellow lines along one side and vehicles parked nose to tail on the other.

The Area car was double parked right outside of number 15b, making an already difficult situation even worse. Already vehicles were trying to reverse back the way they had come. It wouldn't get any better as the day progressed. The narrow road needed to be blocked off at both ends to non-essential vehicles. Marlowe was surprised someone hadn't shown the imitative to have it done already. He only had one option and double parked the Mondeo on the double yellows directly behind the squad car

'Get on the radio and have this bloody road closed,' he told the uniformed officer standing outside the house -

trying to hide his smoke in the cup of his hand. 'And be a bit more discreet,' he nodded to the constable's hand, after all he had done the same when he was in uniform. Embarrassed at being caught out smoking on duty, he dropped the cigarette to the floor and kicked it down a drain.

Jenny opened the boot of Marlowe's car and took out two pair of latex overshoes, she passed a pair to the DCI, who stood on the pavement looking at the drab property. It reminded him of his childhood home down Walcott Street on Hessle Road. A two up and two down red brick terraced house, with a slate roof and windows that rattled in the wind. Like Marlowe's childhood home there was no front garden and just a concrete yard as big as a postage stamp around the back, where his parents hung the tin bath on the wall. Depressing. Marlowe took out his cigarettes and walked across to the opposite side of the road from the house. 'You go in, Jenny, be with you in a minute,' he said holding up the cigarette. He saw the constable look over and raise his eyebrows. 'I'm the Boss,' was all he said as he put the cigarette between his lips.

Jenny nodded and ducked underneath the flapping blue and white crime scene tape that had been strung up between the lampposts on either side of the street. At the doorway to the property she put on the protective footwear and a pair of latex gloves. She didn't want a bollocking when the Crime Scene Manager and her team arrived. More flashing lights were heading down from the direction of Newland Avenue.

The DCI finished his cigarette and dropped it down the same drain as the uniform. He smiled at the constable as he entered the house.

'Where are we, Jenny?' he shouted from the small hallway.

'Upstairs, first door on the right. The door was open when uniform found him.'

The DCI carefully made his way up the threadbare carpet, at the same time pulling on a pair of Nitrile gloves. The flat was the complete opposite to that of Robert Bacuss's bachelor pad, not a piece of designer furniture in sight. Thin rugs on the floor covering the lino, a Lenovo laptop was on the plastic topped coffee table, along with a half cup of instant coffee that was growing penicillin. A soggy settee that had seen better days stood back against one wall. There was, however, the obligatory flat screen television fixed to the wall above the ancient fire grate.

Unlike most student accommodation Harrison had the luxury of a separate bedroom and a miniscule shower room. The kitchen was shared, and downstairs.

Jenny was in the bedroom kneeling on the floor next to the bed.

'I've sent for the Medical Examiner,' she said as she sensed Marlowe looking over her shoulder. Harrison lay fully clothed on top of the already made bed, he looked peaceful she thought - as peaceful as a corpse could look.

'Looks as if some has deliberately laid him out, he smells of something though - can't make out what.' She said as she stood up.

'Smells like engine or gearbox oil to me. Better not touch anything just yet. Have a good snoop around.'

Jenny began the search of the small flat. Marlowe resumed his position next to the bed. Going against his own words he took out a pen from his pocket and started gently prodding. Blood had seeped around Harrison's head, like a crimson halo on the pillow. The lack of blood at the scene convinced Marlowe the lad had died somewhere else and been brought to his current resting place. Why bring him home? Was one of the questions he asked himself - maybe it wasn't murder, killers don't usually treat their victims with any respect.

'How are you getting on, Jenny?' His knees creaked, as he placed his arms on the edge of the bed and eased himself upright. He grunted under his breath as other involuntary twinges made an audible presence when he straightened his back.

'You say something, sir?'

'How are you getting on?'

'No, thought you said something after that.'

'Nothing worth repeating.' As of late his aches and pains seemed to be getting worse, he put it down as an age thing and popped the occasional paracetamol when he had to.

Jenny came out of the small shower room, pulling off the Nitrile gloves. 'Nothing in there that shouldn't be. Same goes for the living room, mind there is a tobacco tin with an ounce or so of weed in it.'

'Jonno said he was a bit of a dope head.'

Loud footsteps bounded up the stairs - it could only be a copper. A head poked around the doorway. 'Crime Scene Examiners have arrived, sir, thought best to let you know.'

'Thanks, cheers. Okay, Jenny, let's make ourselves scarce before we get ourselves a bollocking from Karina, goodness knows what she'll be like.'

'Traumatised I should think!'

Karina Taylor was without doubt a first class Crime Scene Manager, not only proficient at the management side of things, but also an expert when it came to being hands on. But she had one failing - she didn't like looking into the eyes of the dead. She thought it like looking into the soul and it fazed her more than she cared to admit.

On the street once again, Marlowe had an important decision to make, have another smoke or a chewy mint. The cigarettes won - again.

'Do you know what's really peeing me off?'

'Enlighten me,' Marlowe said as he flicked the wheel on the Zippo and lit up, he noticed the uniform standing by the door watching, longingly. Standing there with his smoke, he watched the crime scene people unload their gear, aluminium box after box from their van onto the pavement.

'This lad, Harrison, he was the closest thing we had to a lead. If anyone knew where Robert Bacuss is, it would have been him, now we're back to bloody square one,' she ranted, obviously frustrated.

'Precisely, the question is what do we do now?'

'And another thing,' said the DS venting her frustration. 'If he was murdered somewhere else, why bring him home to bed? I just don't get it.'

'A killer with a conscience? Maybe, just maybe, he came home himself. Got into a brawl, got himself a nasty bang on the head, popped a couple of pills and went to get his head down, and never woke up?' Marlowe enjoyed playing devil's advocate, it prompted his junior colleagues to think outside the box.

'Not very likely though, is it?'

'We'll have to wait and see what the Medical Examiner has to say. Someone has sent for him?'

'I did, he's tied up at the minute, be here as soon as he can.'

'The parrot needs tying up and dropping into the river.' The DCI and Owen Harrison never saw eye to eye, always accusing Marlowe of interfering with the body - even when he hadn't. 'Come on, let's get back to the nick, you can buy me a cup of coffee. He stubbed the cigarette in the gutter. 'Then see if we can come up with some answers not more questions.'

Chapter 19

Rab was really beginning to lose the plot. Had he been in his cell for days - weeks? In reality, it had only been four days, four very long days. Both Paul and Eddie had made appearances day and night. The violence of the first couple of days had stopped and they never came empty handed. He had read enough crime novels and watched enough films, he knew how kidnappers treated their victims, he counted himself lucky at least he was well fed and watered. But still he wished Bruce Willis, in his white vest would come rushing to his rescue.

'How is Mick involved in all this?' Rab asked as he unwrapped his double cheeseburger.

'He's not.' A short, curt response.

'Yeah, but he's the one who...'

'Look, Mick isn't involved, not now anyway - okay?'

'Been in touch with my old man yet?' Paul gave him the "look". 'Only asking.'

'Oh for fuck's sake will you give up with the questions? It won't be long now and you'll be out of my hair once and for all.'

The sooner Eddie arranged a meeting with Stephens the better, the way he was feeling he'd have settled on swapping Rab for a packet of fags.

'That's all I wanted to know,' Rab answered dejectedly.

'Right, you got enough grub and drink? Cos I might not get back till tomorrow, with a bit of luck I'll have the answer you're looking for.'

Rab didn't speak, what was the point he would only get told to "shut the fuck up". He resigned himself to another lonely night in his cell with the girlie mags.

Chapter 20

Things were going from bad to worse. Marlowe wished he and Archie were still in Whitby away from the mess. The one person who, at this stage of their investigation could have thrown some light onto the whereabouts of Robert Bacuss was dead - possibly murdered.

'More bad news, Phil,' Dave Gowan said as he entered Marlowe's glass partitioned office.

'As if I'm not pissed as it is.' He took off his reading glasses and dropped them on the desk. Sat back and rubbed his tired eyes with his knuckles. Gowan dropped an early copy of the evening edition of the Hull Daily Mail on the desk beside Marlowe's glasses.

'Should put them back on.'

He did, giving them a quick clean with his tie first.

Marlowe read the headlines of the *Hull Daily Mail*. **"Prominent business man's son kidnapped."**

'For God's sake,' Marlowe threw the paper down in frustration - then picked it up again and read aloud.

"... According to a reliable source the police have little or no information as to the whereabouts of Robert Bacuss..."

'Who the hell is this reliable source, if it's anyone in the nick I'll kick their arse into next week.'

'Let's be honest about this, it's not likely to be anyone in the nick is it? I bet you a pound to a pinch of shit, it's your pal Shag Pile behind the whole thing.'

'Yeah, you're probably right, it's his style. But what the hell is he hoping to achieve by putting it out there?' Marlowe's phone rang, he picked up the receiver and slammed the handset back down again without answering.

Gowan raised his eyebrows. 'Frustration I suppose, like us. I reckon he thinks it will give us a kick up the arse.'

'Well, he's wrong, I will not be intimidated by a jumped up fucking carpet salesman - and I'll fucking tell him that.'

After visiting Shag Pile Charlie and reading him the riot act Marlowe headed home to Beverley. The Mondeo crunched down the gravel path to the secure parking compound. He could hear Archie barking recognition as he re-locked the compound gates. Harry from the Old Lock Keeper's cottage had returned Archie to the *Daisy* early.

'Alright, pal,' Marlowe said to Archie as the dog danced around and between his legs when he entered the galley. 'Ready for your tea?' He asked, kneeling down making a fuss of the mutt. Marlowe stood up and opened the cupboard where Archie's food was kept. 'Won't be a minute, pal,' he opened the tin and scraped half the contents into Archie's bowl.

Archie was always his priority when he returned home, made sure he was fed and watered before himself. When his companion was done, the pair then ventured onto the Beckside. He sat on his usual concrete mooring bollard, smoking, while Archie did his sniffing and peeing. A

151

familiar figure was walking down the towpath towards him. It was Joyce, Harry's wife and she was carrying something, Marlowe had a good idea what it would be - his evening meal.

'Thought you might like a proper meal for a change instead of some microwaved frozen rubbish,' she said as she passed over a plate of homemade meat pie and vegetables.

'Joyce, whatever would I do without you? How's the arthritis these days?'

'Fair to middling, better some days than others,' she said, folding her arms across her chest, like his grandmother used to. 'So, that ex-missus of yours and her blokes made the papers. Not your case is it - the kidnap?'

'Unfortunately, yes, one job I could have done without. This dinner smells good,' he said, trying to change the subject. Joyce had a way of getting things out of you, things you didn't want to tell her.

'Are you any nearer finding the lad?' It was as bad as being questioned by the press. 'Sorry, I can't tell you anything that's not in the paper - not being awkward, it's just procedure.'

'I understand, now go and have your tea before it dries up, just pop it in the, err,' she hesitated a few seconds, 'microwave for a few minutes. See you in the morning,' she turned and headed home.

'Thanks for this, Joyce,' he called to her back and received a wave in response. Marlowe finished his second cigarette and gradually eased Archie back on his long lead.

When his dinner warmed he sat in the dinette area of the *Daisy's* saloon and enjoyed his first home cooked meal in a while. With his meal finished he put on his jacket, checked the pockets for his cigarettes and lighter, then with a glass of Merlot in hand, Marlowe and Archie returned to the towpath. The smoking was getting way beyond a habit, it had become a ritual. Once again, he sat on the bollard smoking, drinking and pondering, while Archie did - what Archie did. He was due an early night.

'Robert Arthur Bacuss that's who I am, and I will not let these bastards beat me and I *will* walk out of here.' He said the words out loud, but didn't really have the conviction to believe them, in reality he doubted that he would ever get out of the place. He'd never heard of a kidnap victim being released alive or sane. He was hardly a priority for an SAS assault team, even if they did know where he was being held. Over the previous days he'd had plenty of time to think - he remembered reading somewhere about Stockholm Syndrome, whereby the victim shows empathy, even sympathy with their abductor. Rab certainly didn't have any empathy with the bastards that had kidnapped him and broken his nose - but if that was the way to play it he would.

If trying to con himself to freedom was the way to go, so be it, he would give it his best shot, but who would be the best to "play" Paul or Eddie. Paul was definitely the leader, the stronger willed of the two. Eddie came over as the hard-man, but always gave the appearance of not wanting to be there. Maybe he would give Eddie a try, after all, what did he have to lose? He was on the losing side anyway.

Rab lay back against the wall dozing, hearing the bolt drawn on his cell door. He rubbed his eyes and sat forward on the edge of the bed. It was Eddie.

'Eddie, good to see you,' Rab forced the words out, he was going to add mate into the greeting but thought maybe that was going too far.

This wasn't the response he was expecting. 'Brought you some supplies.' He put a plastic carrier bag down on the bed.

'Heard from my old man yet?' The biker shook his head. 'Ah well can't be much longer can it?'

Eddie walked across the room and stood resting his back against the base unit. 'What the fuck's up with you being all nice and friendly?'

'Fed up - fed up of the agro. No point in kicking off at every opportunity is there?'

'Nope, won't get you out any quicker.'

'That's what I reckoned, not that I'm giving in mind.' He started to rummage in the carrier bag. 'You been partners with Armstrong long?'

'A good while now, why?'

'Well, it seems to me that he thinks he's the one in charge, but I know different, it's you that really pulls the strings an idiot can see that.' Rab played to Eddie's ego as he opened a packet of crisps and offered the bag. Eddie didn't respond any further and started for the door. 'Can't let me have a smoke can you, I can hardly set the place alight with you here?'

Eddie stopped and took his tobacco pouch from his pocket. 'Can't do any harm I suppose.' He rolled a thin cigarette and passed it over.

'Cheers,' Rab put the rollie between his lips. Eddie reached across and flicked his light, Rab sucked greedily, then sat back on the bed resting against the wall. 'Phew, thanks, Eddie, I needed that.'

'No problem.' A good response.

'Haven't got a beer to go with have you?'

'This isn't a bleedin hotel.' Eddie smiled for the first time. 'I'm off,' he made towards the door.

'Thanks for the food and smoke,' Rab said as Eddie went through the door. 'Shit head,' he added, as the door closed and locked. He pushed back on the bed and rested against the wall. Okay, so Eddie seemed to have mellowed a little, but Rab knew in his heart there wasn't a cat in hell's chance of getting the biker onside, maybe if he'd had six months to work on him, in reality he knew he'd be lucky if he had six days.

Chapter 21

Paul was on tenterhooks, he wasn't looking forward to meeting the man who they hoped would take Bacuss off their hands. He rolled another cigarette, watching the condensation run down the windows in *Fat Sam's*.

'This Stephens, he doesn't know we've had the coppers sniffing around does he?'

'Give me some fucking credit Paul!'

'Yeah, well, just asking.'

The pair sat in silence for a few minutes. Eddie because he knew what to expect of Stephens. Paul, well he didn't know the first thing about the bloke.

The silence was broken when the door opened and slammed shut. It was Stephens.

He stood looking around the near empty café, smiled at Eddie then pulled out a chair and sat down. 'And you are?' he asked Paul as he took out a pack of cigarettes.

'Armstrong - Paul Armstrong.' No one offered to shake hands, just nodded.

Stephens spoke with a cigarette hanging from his mouth. 'You do know this meeting never took place? You don't know me, you've never heard of me - you deny everything. If that's agreeable, we can continue?'

Paul and Eddie didn't speak, nodding their agreement. Paul took out his lighter and reached over to light Stephens's cigarette.

He backed away. 'Trying to give them up.' Derek Stephens sat back in his seat, rocking on the back legs. Fat Sam came over and slammed down a mug of tea in front of him. Not receiving any thanks. Stephens sipped from the mug. He didn't look the type of bloke to get involved in the abduction business, or any other dubious business for that matter. Judging from the way he was dressed, in a two piece suit with a shirt and tie, he didn't look anything other than a businessman. He was ultra careful and discreet, never got his hands dirty. That was left to the people he employed – people who knew how to keep their mouths shut. He only employed people who, if they did fall foul of the law would deny ever knowing him. They knew their families would be taken care of while they did their time. When the odds of serving prison time were weighed up with the good money Stephens paid, it was a no brainer.

'So, Eddie tells me you have some merchandise you would like me to take off your hands?' He looked across the table at Paul. 'According to our mutual friend here, you want seven grand for the goods, right?

'We need a quick deal...' Paul was cut off mid sentence.

'Please don't interrupt,' he had one of those voices that screamed authority. 'How much am I likely to gross on the closure of the transaction?'

'Twenty, thirty, forty grand, you can name your own price. We just want rid ASAP.' Paul replied in a low voice as he leaned across the table resting on his elbows.

Stephens sat back in his chair, held the palm of his hand out in front of him. He didn't like people invading his space. Sitting back in his chair, he studied each face in turn. After a lengthy pause he spoke. 'I've come to a decision.' Paul and Eddie looked at each other, this was it end game, now they could start living their lives again. 'I'm not interested.'

Paul slammed the flat of his hands on the table. 'Why the hell not?'

'It seems to me you're a bit too keen - hot property I'm thinking, right?

'Maybe, but look at the money you could make.' Paul was almost pleading.

'I don't have to explain myself to you.' He pushed back his chair, stood up and straightened his tie. Smiled down on Paul and Eddie and then left without another word.

Paul and Eddie sat there not comprehending the situation. 'What the fuck just happened?'

Eddie shrugged his shoulders. 'You heard the man, he's not interested.'

'Now what?'

Eddie shrugged again.

'That bloke is something else. How the hell do you know people like that?'

'A long story, through a bloke who knew a bloke, like I said it's a long story,' he turned and shouted over his shoulder. 'Sam, bring us another couple of teas.' Then he turned back to face his partner. 'If we're gonna be stuck with him I reckon we should move him, sharpish.'

'Why's that?'

'Once the coppers start asking about Mick, I don't reckon on it being long before they come sniffing around the yard.'

'Got anywhere in mind?'

'There's the old air-raid shelter at the bottom of me mam's garden.'

Pauls's mother lived in a detached Victorian bungalow on the edge of the village of North Ferriby, just to the west of the city. The more he thought about it the more he was convinced the location was perfect. The bungalow was set back a good distance from the road with no close neighbours, and benefited from a long garden, that almost stretched to the bank of the River Humber. Hidden amongst the long grass was an Anderson Shelter, a relic left over from the second world war.

Eddie was concerned. 'This shelter, don't you think it's a bit risky?'

'You mean, mam? No worries there, she's as deaf as a post and hardly ever leaves the house, as for the garden she's never been down to the shelter for years. So what do you think?'

Eddie had a plan of his own, unbeknown to his partner he had already made a call to Bacuss. The drop was to be soon, sooner rather than later. 'So let's do it, as you said it won't be long before Mr Plod comes back with a search warrant. Once we get him shifted, I'll go back and sort out the lockup, we don't want coppers to link it to Bacuss,' Eddie told his partner.

'Good thinking.'

Eddie made sure he was first into the lockup, he took a rag from his pocket and wiped clean any surface, he touched erasing his finger prints as he went. Any fresh prints would belong to Paul.

Rab heard the lock opening, wrapped a blanket around his shoulders, he shuffled forward and sat on the edge of the bed. 'Ah, I guess my old man's come up with the cash then?' he said as he stood up pulling the blanket tighter for warmth. The question fell on deaf ears.

'Come on,' Paul ordered as he grabbed Rab around the bicep.

'Ow, go steady man,' he complained as he was led through the workshop. 'Won't miss this place one fucking bit.' Rab didn't argue.

The scrap yard van was parked directly outside the lockup entrance, the side sliding door open.

'In you go,' he took a deep breath of fresh air before climbing in the back, he was just pleased to be out of the soundproof room. Still with the blanket wrapped around, he crawled across the floor and sat on the spare wheel.

Paul climbed in the back after him. 'Put your arms behind you,' he said, grabbing the skinny wrists in one shovel sized hand pulling them around Rab's back and taped them together.

'Come on, Paul, there's no need for this... ow... go steady man.' Before he could protest further a strip of tape was then stuck over his mouth. It was then he realised that maybe he wasn't being set free. Rab started to twist and turn and kicked out at Armstrong.

'Keep bloody still. Eddie, grab his legs.'

Eddie leaned in through the open door and tried to get a hold of the flaying legs only to receive a boot to the face. 'You little shit.' Roughly he grabbed both feet while Paul bound them together with sticky tape.

Rab was still desperately writhing about trying to free himself as the van door closed, shutting him in complete darkness. All he wanted to do was go home, but hopes of freedom faded with every passing minute.

Paul drove the Transit van along English Street and took the Freetown Way junction on to the A63, Clive Sullivan Way and headed west towards the village of North Ferriby, a fifteen minute drive away.

As they approached the village small holdings and detached bungalows came into view in the van's headlights.

'Which one is it?' Armstrong asked as he peered into the darkness.

'Not far, slow down. That one, it's that one the third bungalow on the left.'

He slowed and dropped down a gear, turned into the overgrown drive, Paul referred to the place as a bungalow, but Eddie thought it more akin to the small holding they had just passed and thought that could only be a good thing. The actual dwelling was a pre-war bungalow separated from the drive by a wide expanse of overgrown weeds. Armstrong drove at a crawl down the overgrown rutted driveway, all the time Rab was being tossed every which way in the back.

Eddie was surprised at the length of the drive, it must have been one hundred metres before the van's headlights picked out the earth mound of the Anderson shelter.

Perfect he thought, it couldn't be seen from the bungalow, a good distance from the road and neighbouring properties. Armstrong killed the engine and the van stopped with a jolt, rocking on the ruts and bouncing about its occupant in the back.

'What do you think?' asked Marriot.

'It'll do the job, you sure your mam never comes down this way?'

'With her arthritis, she's lucky to walk to the front door - that's on a good day.'

'Right, let's go take a look,' he said and climbed down from the van, picking his way through the undergrowth. The shelter had been built in 1940 for protection against air-raids. Anderson shelters were supplied as kits, basically sheets of corrugated iron preformed into curved sections. A large, deep hole would be dug in the garden, with sheets lining the side and the curved section forming a room. The entire thing would then be covered with earth or sandbags to offer meagre protection from falling bombs.

The years had taken their toll on the shelter, it was barely visible through the overgrowth, it was two steps down to the rotting timber entrance door. Paul struggled to pull open the door, the rusting hinges hadn't been greased in years. 'Let me have a go,' said Eddie as he grabbed the metal handle. After a few minutes of tugging and swearing the timber door juddered its way open. 'Bloody hell,' Eddie almost gagged as the smell of damp and decay came flooding out.

'Should be a light switch somewhere on the right, Gramps used the place as a workshop at one time.'

Eddie found the switch, luckily the electric still worked and a dim bulb encased in a protective wire cage flickered into life. 'Fucking hell,' Paul jumped back, a rat the size of a small dog scurried over his boots. 'We can't keep him in here - look at the state of the fucking place, I wouldn't keep chickens in here - or rats come to that.' The wooden boarded floor was rotten and creaked underfoot. Rivulets of water ran down the corrugated metal sides, the place wasn't fit to keep anything in - alive that is. The wartime bunks had been removed and replaced with a heavy wooden workbench and shelving that was struggling to stay fixed to the walls.

Eddie took a further step inside. 'I've got a bad feeling about this mate - a very bad feeling.' He stepped inside. 'What's them marks around the walls?' About three feet from the floor a green and rust coloured mark circled the metal sheeting.

'Remember last year when we had the tidal flood? This part of the garden flooded and that's how high up the shelter the water came.'

'So we just leave him in here?'

'The place is like a fucking dungeon, what'll we do chain him to the wall?'

'Why not? Look, Eddie, it'll only be another day, two max – he can survive for that long.'

'Okay two days max – then what will we do, let him walk away? For fuck's sake he knows who we are, if he says anything you'll never get your pub back.'

'Let me worry about that.' The thought had crossed Paul's mind - more than once. He wasn't a killer - never had been. But the more he thought about he wanted his pub back the more desperate he became and if that meant Rab never left the Anderson shelter so be it. 'You just make sure you've got your passport ready and some sun screen packed.'

Eddie didn't feel as if he owed the lad in the van any favours, he was just the means to an end - but this? Reluctantly, he answered. 'Don't have much choice do we?'

Paul shrugged his shoulders in response. 'We doing this or what?' He picked up a damp, foul smelling hessian sack off the workbench. 'Best shove this over his head, we don't want him freaking, he'll do that soon enough.' Paul led the way back to the transit and slid open the side door. Rab saw the sack in his hand and immediately started kicking and writhing about and shaking his head as Paul tried to place it over his head. 'Keep fucking still or I'll batter yer,' he said as he grabbed Rab by the hair, eventually managed to shroud his head in the rotting material.

Eddie grabbed Rab by the feet and dragged him across the van floor. All the time the lad tried to shout and scream through the tape across his mouth. Paul took a hold of his shoulders. Between them, they manhandled the struggling gambler, stumbling over the uneven ground and undergrowth. Paul walked backwards down the three steps into the shelter. Rab twisted and tried to kick out with his bound legs. Eddie wasn't happy as he grabbed the legs tighter stumbling down the steps after Paul.

Carefully treading their way over the rotting floor, they edged their way to the far end of the mausoleum and dropped the lad to the floor. Rab, winded, grunted as he hit the wooden flooring. Without speaking to Rab they retraced their steps, slammed the door shut and replaced the padlock.

'Like I said two days max, he can manage that long then I'll give him back to his old man - maybe,' Paul said as they picked their way through the overgrown weeds.

With difficulty he reversed the van back down the rutted driveway towards the road. No lights could be seen through the closed curtains of the bungalow.

Eddie peered through the side window. 'Looks like your mam's all tucked up.'

'Way past her bedtime. You ready for a pint?'

'Think I'll give it a miss and sort the lockup out.'

'I'll give you a hand...'

Eddie was quick off the mark. 'Na, I can manage, just drop me off at the yard to get the cleaning stuff. You could shift the mattress though, dump it.'

'No problem mate. This time tomorrow we'll be quids in.'

Between them, they loaded the mattress used by Rab into the van, all the time being careful letting Armstrong take the lead, his fingerprints and DNA were everywhere, he had worn a pair of Armstrong's work gloves over his rubber cleaning gloves. So far so good, he was convinced he had done a good clean up job with the bleach, not too much - not too little, but enough to leave a significant trace of Rab's and Armstrong's DNA.

Job done, still wearing the work gloves he secured the lockup and headed home - tomorrow was to be a big day.

Chapter 22

Eddie Marriot's cousin, Gordon, went into work as usual. He was always early for his shift. This was the day the "parcel" was due to arrive in the Royal Mail's, Sutton Fields sorting office. Gordon was lucky, he had been asked to do some overtime before his shift in the sorting department to cover sick leave. He couldn't believe his luck, it made things a lot easier. Gordon drove his tired Ford Fiesta into the depot car park and parked up, he wished the shift was already over. He managed a cup of tea in the canteen without gagging before his shift started. Even at 5.30am the banter between the posties was flowing back and forth thick and fast, with each and every one of them having the piss taken out of them at one time or another.

'Wot you up to after you've finished?' someone yelled across the sorting room floor to Gordon.

'Doin wot I allus duz when we knock off, gooin 'ome to get me ed down for a couple of hours.' All the time he looked for the package that would be wrapped in a green builder's rubble bag. The idea being, the green would make it relatively easy to spot when it was put into his mate's packet-tub - if he didn't spot it first.

It was a busy morning and the packets and parcels came fast. Gordon was beginning to think maybe it hadn't been posted at all - then he saw it, it was on the next "yorkie" to be unloaded. He was sure that the police had not informed the management to look out for it. If they had the duty manager would have been on the sorting office floor, keeping an eye on things.

Gordon wandered over to the "yorkie," grabbed an armful of packets and casually began tossing them into the individual postie's tubs - a quick check of the address and the green package went in his own tub, soon to be covered by others packets and parcels. An hour later the sorting was finished and he was back on his mail fitting. A sly look around then he quickly tucked the tightly bundled green package into the front pouch of one of his bags, the one he'd take with him when he started his "walk".

A quick fag break was needed. In the smoker's shed he sat on the narrow bench and rolled up and lit his smoke. He took out his mobile and sent a text message to Eddie, "Got it, see you later". Once his smoke was finished, he went back inside and carried on sorting the rest of his mail.

An hour and a half later, his mail sorted and the fitting clear, Gordon loaded his bag into the front carrier of his bicycle and his next two bags into the cycle panniers. It was the first time since arriving at work that morning, that his heart went back to some sort of normal rhythm, as he cycled out of the sorting office yard. He cycled along Rotterdam Road with his mobile glued to his ear.

'Eddie, it's me,' he said as he negotiated the heavy balanced cycle with his free hand.

Gordon could hear the relief in Eddie's voice as he spoke at the other end. 'I've been having kittens waiting here, any problems? He had been sitting with his mobile in his hand for the past hour.

'Nope, I've got the package, it's all going according to plan, no problems at all. It'll take me about thirty minutes to get to, just a minute,' he said as the cycle wobbled, '... oh shit,' the top heavy cycle went over. Gordon dropped his mobile as he fell into the road - under the front wheels of a thirty ton articulated lorry.

'Gordon... Gordon what the fuck's going on... Gordon answer me.' The only sound Eddie heard was the sound of screeching brakes and the crunching sound of metal as the heavy wheels went over Gordon's cycle. Eddie was puzzled, wondering why the conversation had stopped mid-sentence, he hung up the call. There was nothing to do but wait for Gordon to call back.

Fifteen minutes - thirty minutes, when it reached forty five minutes he pressed Gordon's speed dial number. The call was picked up. 'Gordon what the fuck are you playing at?' he almost screamed down the line.

'Who's calling please?'

'Who the fucks that, what are you doing on Gordon's phone?'

'This is the Police, please... who are you, it's important?'

'Eddie, Eddie Marriot I'm Gordon's cousin - I'm waiting for a call from him.' He couldn't believe it. What was a copper doing with Gordon's mobile.

'Unfortunately, Mr Marriot has been involved in a road traffic accident,' said the Traffic Policeman.

'What's happened - is he okay?'

'I'm very sorry, sir, I can't tell you anything more until the next of kin have been informed.'

Eddie hung up and almost dropped his mobile, his hands shook as he tried to put the phone in his pocket. What did the copper mean, "next of kin had been informed?" What was that all about - shit. He pulled himself together, put on his jacket and crash helmet, fired his 1000cc Honda motorcycle and set off for Gordon's house.

Chapter 23

'Have you heard anything from Bacuss?' DI Gowan asked as Marlowe came into the squad room.

'Heard anything, I went around last night when we knocked off, I told him he was well out of order. A lot of good it did, he just called in, and told me, and I quote, "a lot of useless bastards" we are.' The DCI said as he put his briefcase on the floor, pulled up a chair and sat down. 'Mind you he might have something about us being useless.' Despite all their efforts they still had very little to go on.

'Well, while you were at the Stats meeting there's been a development - of sorts.'

'What kind of development, progress I hope?' He removed his jacket and hung it over a spare chair.

'Early this morning a postman was involved in a fatal RTC - flattened under the front wheels of a thirty six ton lorry and tractor unit.'

'Hell, poor bloke - but what's the connection?' Marlowe asked as he rubbed his tired eyes, it had been an early meeting and very boring he was in the need of caffeine and nicotine.

'This particular postman had an unusual package in his bag,' Gowan gave a slight smile. 'Ok, maybe I shouldn't be smiling, but the wheels not only went over him, they also went over his pouch and spread mail across the road, amongst those parcels that were scattered was not the run of the mill second class parcel.'

'Come on Dave, spit it out?'

'It was only stuffed with money - twenty grand to be precise.'

The DCI slammed the palms of his hands down. Gowan was quick, he managed to save his mug of congealed coffee before it spilled over the desk. 'Bloody Shag Pile! I might have known. Why can't that bloody man leave well alone?'

'What's significant is the postie's name was Gordon Evans, he's - was the cousin of Eddie Marriot, Armstrong's partner in the scrap yard.' Gowan stood up and stretched. 'Fancy a coffee?'

'That *is* what I call significant, and yes to the coffee. This could be the break we've been waiting for,' he said as he rocked back in his seat. 'Robert, mates with Harrison - one missing one dead. Armstrong and Marriot plus the postie with twenty grand in his pouch.' Marlowe dropped his chair back down. 'Bloody man, I despair honestly.'

Gowan left the office and paid a visit to the vending machine in the corridor. 'Don't have the tea, sir,' a uniformed officer said as he walked past.

'Thanks for the heads up,' the DI replied as he fed coins into the machine.

Back in the squad room the conversation continued. 'So, now we've got something that links them together. Marriot tied in with Armstrong, the money and what's more what we think was engine oil on the body of Michael Harrison. Have we had the forensic report back?'

Gowan shook his head. 'I'll chase them up.'

Marlowe sat quiet for a moment or two, then exploded - again. 'What the hell was Shag Pile doing sending twenty grand through the bloody post?'

'Beggars belief,' Gowan shook his head.

'I've had enough of his interference, have the idiot brought in. This coffee tastes like tea!' he said as he spat it back in the cup. 'And get that package dusted for prints before he's brought in.'

'It's been done.'

Chapter 24

'Okay, you're good to go,' DI Gowan said to Jonno as he came into the squad room waving a piece of paper in his hand. 'Got you a search warrant for the scrap yard and associated premises, including the pub.'

'Thanks Dave, what swung it?'

'The post mortem report on Harrison, engine oil on the lad's clothing and Armstrong's DNA all over him.'

'How did you manage to get a sample?'

'Picked up a fag end he dropped.'

'Jonno, how unethical,' Marlowe said grinning.

'So, you betting on murder?'

'Not necessary at this stage, could have been an accident.'

'If it was an accident, why put the lad to bed?'

'Put there - put himself there? We don't know anything, pick Marriot up and we'll find out in the interview. Any bother, arrest him.'

'Fair enough, I'll grab Lee and a couple of uniforms, on second thoughts I'll make it three plus a dog handler for that bloody great long haired German Shepherd that roams the yard.'

'With a bit of luck we'll find something in the yard.'

Jonno, with his hands in his pockets, stood before the small team he had assembled to carry out the raid on the scrap yard. 'Right, settle down,' he said above the chattering voices. 'This is how it's going to work, from a health and safety point of view the scrap yard is full of hazards - it's a bloody nightmare. You all know what scrap yards are like? Well, this one is worse, so be bloody careful. If any of you come back and put a claim in for injury the Super will haul me over the coals. Okay?'

'So, Jonno, if I do have an accident or summat who should I sue?' asked one of the uniforms assigned to the small team.

'Pete, don't be a twat, you know what I mean. Just don't go and break your bloody neck, that's all I'm saying,' the response produced a few laughs. Pete always tried to be the joker - his humour wasn't always appreciated.

'Chas, I want you to position yourself outside the lockup,' Chas nodded. PC Charles Henderson, was just the man to stand guard, a broad shouldered imposing bloke and threatening with it. He was also pretty good if things became physical. 'Lee and I will go in first with the dog handler to make sure the Shepherd is chained and contained.' Lee gave him a look that more or less said "do I have to?" he wasn't a great dog lover at the best of times. 'Once we know the dog's secure, that's when you start the search.'

Fifteen minutes later the small convoy made their silent approach to the scrap yard. The group were in good humour as they gathered around the lead car - deep down one or two were hoping for some aggro.

'Chas, keep out the way and keep your eyes on the lockup,' he nodded to the unit across the road. 'I've just got a feeling about the place, if anyone approaches to open up give me a call on the AirWave then arrest them. When we've finished in the yard, we'll come back and join you.' He turned to face the remaining officers. 'Okay, let's go.'

They climbed back into their vehicles for the two hundred metre journey. Two squad cars and the dog handler's van parked across the entrance to the yard, leaving no vehicle access - more importantly no exit.

Lee gave Jonno a worried look when he heard the scrap yard pooch howling somewhere out of sight.

'Wimp!' Jonno said as he gave the dog handler a nod to take the lead.

'What the fuck do you lot want now?' A threatening voice demanded to know. The voice belonged to Armstrong, he was heading towards them. Eddie Marriot was a pace behind.

'We have a warrant to search the place.' Jonno passed over the search warrant.

'On what fucking grounds,' he asked as he passed the warrant back without reading. Marriot, looking furtive - took a step back.

It didn't go un-noticed. 'Where's the dog?' Lee asked, his eyes scanning the yard.

Marriot laughed. 'Somewhere around,' he turned and started to walk back to the office. 'Let me know when you're done,' he said, with his back towards them.

'Mr Marriot!' Jonno called, he was following Armstrong to the office, he stopped dead in his tracks. 'We'd like you to come down the station to answer a few questions.'

Armstrong gave a half glance over his shoulder. He was stunned briefly, he wondered if it was worth taking a chance - leg it down the yard and scale the fence. He decided it really wasn't an option, turned and walked towards the officers. 'Put him in one of the cars and take him back to the station.'

Then the search began with officers spreading over the yard, but not until the dog handler confirmed the German Shepherd was actually chained securely. While Lee and the uniforms carried out the search of the yard, Jonno and a constable made a start inside the portable office. Meanwhile the search of the scrap yard was proving to be a nightmare. As Jonno predicted the place was a health and safely nightmare. Progress was painfully slow, access beyond the immediate vicinity was an impossibility.

'Alright lads, take it steady looks like some of these heaps could topple any minute,' he said as he warily eyed up the vehicles piled four or five high. Reluctantly the search was drawn to a close, almost as quickly as it started.

Armstrong sat in his chair behind the desk as they began. Drawers were emptied of their contents, cupboards opened. 'I hope you're going to put things back where you found them,' he said sarcastically. No one responded, they just carried on. 'Finished?' he asked when he could sense their frustration. 'Could have told you you'd be wasting your time.'

Jonno looked Armstrong in the eyes. 'Nearly, we'd like to have a look at the building next door.'

Armstrong rummaged through the contents of his desk drawer which was now spread across his desk, picked up a bunch of keys and passed them over. 'Be my guest.'

Jonno was disappointed, he was hoping for some resistance to the request, he knew then they'd find nothing. Regardless the search had to be made. 'In the meantime, Mr Armstrong, I'd like you to go with PC James here to the station to answer a few more questions.'

Armstrong didn't appear to be too worried and followed the uniform to a waiting squad car.

Lee, wearing protective gloves turned the key in the heavy security padlock, released the asp and slid open the sturdy timber door along the metal track. 'Wow,' he said as they entered the motorcycle workshop he looked around at the classic motorcycle spares. 'Some expensive vintage stuff in here.'

'So you're a closet petrol head?'

'No, not me, but I do appreciate some of these old bikes. My old man used to have 1950 BSA 650cc Gold Flash, he bought it as a write-off and rebuilt it. Just look at this,' he said as he pulled a dust sheet of a Royal Enfield Bullet.

'Yeah, well, I'm still no wiser, never was into motor bikes.' He inclined his head towards the door in the far wall. Again Lee went forward and inserted a key in the lock. After a few minutes trial and error the lock clicked open.

'These look new,' he said, studying the door.

'And why fit bolts on this side of the door?' Jonno asked.

'There's only one explanation. To keep something or someone on the other side from getting out,' Lee suggested as he reached up and slid open the top bolt, then repeated the sequence with the remaining bolt.

With a latex gloved hand Jonno pushed open the door and stood looking in. A wire-framed single bed was pushed against one wall, he noted there was no mattress. A kitchen unit with microwave complete with basin and cold water tap. Apart from a few aging posters on the wall the room was empty - stark.

'Not furnished for comfort,' Lee said as he stepped inside. 'Looks too clean.'

Outside they heard a van pull up. It was the CSE's. 'Afternoon boys,' Karina the CSE said as she stood looking into the room. Her protective suit crackling as she moved. 'You do realise you could be standing on evidence?'

Embarrassed Lee almost jumped out of the room. 'Soz.'

'Soz? What are you twelve?' asked Jonno embarrassing Lee even more. 'Is that bleach I can smell,' he asked turning to Karina.

'Yep, I'd say someone has been having a bit of a cleanup. Let's have a look shall we?'

She stepped forward, closed the door and holding a Luminal spray before her as she carefully went further into the room. When Luminol is sprayed evenly it reacts with the iron in haemoglobin and emits a blue glow that can be seen for about thirty seconds, with the glow intensifying in concentrated areas.

'Anything?' Lee shouted through the closed door.

The door opened. 'Oh yes, plenty of blood traces, more consistent in the area in front of the bed frame. 'I'll give the place a thorough going over.' Taking some aluminium foot pads from her box of tricks she placed them strategically and stepped back in the room. 'Right then you two, out,' she told Jonno and Lee. 'Daniel, get some pictures and have, Lee, check for prints,' she yelled through the open door.

'That's our cue to piss off,' Jonno said turning to Lee. 'Let us know if you find anything.'

'No, I'll keep it to myself,' Karina said sarcastically. Jonno didn't rise to the comment, just shook his head as he and Lee left her to her work.

'Where next, the pub?' Lee asked as he headed towards the car.

'Yeah, but we're walking, it's only a couple of streets away, its hardly worth moving the car.'

'You have the keys?'

'No, we're going to break in,' said Jonno jangling the keys in his pocket.

Both officers pulled on Nitrile protective gloves. Jonno put the key in the lock and turned the key and eased the pub door open.

'That polish I can smell?' Asked Lee as they walked into the main bar.

'Someone's gone over the top with a clean up,' Jonno replied as he ran a gloved hand across the bar. 'All spick and span. Go take a look upstairs.'

While Lee checked out the living accommodation, Jonno stood looking around, it was a proper old fashioned boozer. Black and White photographs of the long gone Hull trawlers, the fish market and the old fish dock. He was still admiring the photographs when Lee came thundering down the stairs.

'Nothing up there worth talking about, mind you there's some interesting motor bike mags.'

Jonno shook himself out his nostalgic mood. 'Some place this is, it's a shame these places are having to close.'

'You'll be getting the violins out in a minute,' joked Lee as he went around the back of the bar. 'Time - gentlemen - please,' he called out as he rang an old brass ship's bell hanging from the shelves above the bar.

Jonno smiled, wishing he'd thought of the idea. 'Come on, back room.'

The back room was where the poker game was supposed to have taken place. 'When I was young they used call rooms like this the snug, a place where all the old biddies used to come and natter.

'Looks as clean as the bar. Ouch!' he knocked his hip on the edge of an old wooden table.

'Nice one, Lee,' Jonno said, dropping down on one knee. A poker chip that must have been stuck beneath the table leg had been dislodged. With a gloved hand Jonno picked up the chip.

Lee took a plastic evidence bag from his pocket and passed it over. Jonno dropped the chip inside and sealed the bag. 'Right, lets's get back. We'll leave the rest up to Karina and her misfits.'

Chapter 25

'So where the hell is Robert?' Marlowe asked no one in particular.

'Dead?' Lee answered with another question.

'Not helpful, Lee.'

'I was only saying...'

'Yes, I know, but let's not get ahead of ourselves.'

'The logical thing to do would be to move him,' Jonno added. 'I'm pretty sure Armstrong and Marriot would have had enough savvy to shift him after our first visit to the yard.'

'Lee, trawl further into their backgrounds, see if any other properties show up. They've got to have him somewhere secure.'

'No probs.' Lee immediately started tapping on his keyboard.

'What do you reckon, Dave?' Jonno asked DI Gowan as he dropped the plastic evidence bag containing the poker chip on the DIs desk.

Gowan picked up the bag and turned it over in his hands. 'Don't get too excited, Jonno, all it tells us is that someone dropped a poker chip, we still can't prove young Bacuss was there.' Then passed the bag over to Marlowe. 'Good work Jonno,' Marlowe examined the chip through the plastic. 'Might get a print off it.'

'Not enough though, is it.' Gowan sat back in his chair with his hands folded behind his head. 'I don't rate the chances of pulling a print belonging to Rab.'

'Maybe not, but if forensic can get a print off one of the beer bottles, well, who knows. Has either of them got a record?'

'Marriot was arrested for GBH a couple of years back, nothing since.'

'Then we'll have his prints and DNA on record?' Gowan nodded. 'What about the other one?'

'Armstrong, never been in bother, unusual for a bloke who deals in scrap metal. Suppose there has to be a few honest ones about.'

'I doubt it, probably just that he's never been caught.' The DCI was still holding the plastic bag with the poker chip inside, he dropped it on the desk. 'So which interview room is he in?' Marlowe asked as he cleaned his reading glasses with his tie.

'Who, Armstrong or Marriot?'

'Marriot.'

'He's in three,' Jonno smiled.

'Jonno, please not three, it still stinks of drains in there.'

'Sorry boss, there's leckies working in the other two rooms.' Interview room three had a long standing problem, the smell of drains. For months, if not years the building maintenance team had been trying to get to the source of the problem with no luck.

'What sort of mood is he in?'

'Stressed, he wasn't expecting to be brought in.'

'Far from it.'

'That's good, and he hasn't been told why he's being interviewed?'

'Nope, helping with our enquiries. The custody Sergeant kept him and Armstrong separate.'

'Okay Jonno, let's go and see if he can shed any light onto the whereabouts of young Bacuss and see why his cousin had twenty grand in his pouch.'

'It should be interesting at the least.'

The red light above the door showed the room as being occupied. Jonno opened the door, it wasn't very welcoming - the smell. 'Is the air-con working?' Marlowe asked, wrinkling his nose.

'On and off, sir, more off than on,' the uniformed constable keeping any eye on Marriot, replied as he moved towards the door.

Marriot was pacing back and forth. 'So, you're the one in charge?' He asked as Marlowe entered the room, Jonno close behind.

'I am indeed, Mr Marriot, Detective Chief Inspector Marlowe, I believe you have already met my colleague Detective Constable Lawson. Take a seat, Mr Marriot.'

'I'm alright standing thanks.'

'Mr Marriot - it wasn't a request, sit down.' Marriot fired a look at the DCI showing his annoyance.

He stepped towards the Formica topped table, pulled out a chair. 'Am I under arrest?' he asked as he reluctantly sat down.

'Not as yet,' he turned to Jonno for confirmation, he shook his head. 'But it can be arranged. Now, Mr Marriot, we have one or two questions we would like answers to and we believe you can supply those answers.'

'Well, I hope this won't take long, I've got things to do.'

'That all depends on you, Mr Marriot, and how forthcoming you are.' Marlowe replied as he set out a folder on the table and opened it.

'Just to let you know we will be taping the conversation - okay?'

Marriot nodded. Jonno placed two cassettes in the machine and pressed the record button.

Jonno took the lead. 'Michael Harrison, I believe you knew him?' He leaned forward, resting his elbows on the table.

'Y-e-a-h.'

'You knew him well?' Marlowe asked with his eyes still on the folder.

'As well as - he was more of a mate of Paul's than mine.'

'You mean Paul Armstrong?'

'Who else?'

'How did you get on with Harrison?'

'Alright, I suppose.'

'Define alright,' Jonno told him.

'I mean just that - alright, seemed a decent enough lad – in small doses,' he changed position in his seat.

'So you really didn't get on with him?'

'I didn't say that, he was alright, a nice lad. Once he started at Uni he got a bit above himself, like, a bit of a know it all.'

The DCI gave Jonno a quick look, it was time to broach the subject of Robert Bacuss.

'Fair enough, we'll come back to Harrison shortly. How did you come to meet Robert Bacuss?'

Marriot was momentarily thrown. 'Who?'

'Robert Bacuss, he was a friend of Michael Harrisons.'

'Surely you remember him, you played poker with him a couple of times?'

'Poker, me? I'm the world's worst poker player - sorry, but I think you're mistaking me for someone else. Are we going to be much longer?'

'As long as it takes Mr Marriot,' Marlowe said, head down turning pages.

'In that case I think I'd like a solicitor present.' He was on the ropes.

'That's your prerogative, do you have a legal representative or would you like to have a word with the duty solicitor?' Jonno asked him.

'Do I look the kind of bloke who has a solicitor at his beg and call? The duty brief will do just fine.'

'In that case this interview is suspended at,' Marlowe checked the time on the wall clock. '4.30pm.' Then turned off the tape recorder.

Marriot made to stand up. 'Stay where you are, Mr Marriott, a constable will be with us in a minute to escort you to a cell to wait for your brief - and that may be some time.'

'A cell?' Now he was really worried.

'Usual procedure I assure you.'

Jonno opened the door and the uniform waiting outside entered. 'Escort Mr Marriot to one of our best rooms will you please.' The Officer smiled. Marriot stood up and was escorted away without another word. Everyone was relieved to get into the relative fresh air of the corridor

'How long before we get the DNA results back collected off Harrison?' Marlowe asked once they were back in the corridor.

'The lab said they'd rush them through, but as you know it takes time. You think we got him worried - Marriot?'

'I know we have,' Marlowe replied, as he led the way towards CID.

'Next up, Mr Armstrong.'

'Not before coffee, your turn isn't it, Jonno?'

The DCI walked off, leaving Jonno searching in his pocket for change for the vending machine. For some reason or another it was always his turn when it came to pay.

'Thanks,' Marlowe accepted the coffee, 'how much do I owe you?'

'It's okay, my shout.' It was always Jonno's shout.

Back in the office Marlowe gestured for Jonno to make himself comfortable. 'So, when we get back in there, I suggest we go straight for the jugular and ask him about his cousin.'

'Which reminds me, can I use your phone, best sort him out that brief or we'll be in for a bollocking.'

'Help yourself.'

Jonno picked up the handset and dialled Sergeant Cleeves extension. 'Trevor,' he said into the receiver, 'I'm after a favour please, can you sort a solicitor out for Marriot... yeah I know, another favour I owe you. Cheers.'

'What do we know about Armstrong?'

'As we know there's nothing on the PNC. Landlord or ex-landlord of the Blacksmiths Arms, also in partnership with Marriot in the scrap business. He'd known the dead lad all of his life.'

'So maybe he's the one who took the lad home and laid him out. Let's go and have a word, you ready?' Jonno had barely touched his drink, not that it was worth having. 'Right, where have you iced away Armstrong.'

'He's in a cell already.'

'Bloody hell, Jonno, his brief will...'

Jonno cut him off. 'No its okay, boss, told him the interview rooms weren't all available, maintenance work being carried out. He's not locked in - doors open, cup of tea, he seemed happy enough.'

'Well, let's go and piss on his happiness.'

'Sounds like a plan.'

Armstrong looked to be quite content, enjoying another cup of tea, sitting on the low bed in the cell. He looked the tough guy type, thought the DCI as they stepped into the cell.

'Mr Armstrong will you come with us,' Jonno suggested.

'Where are we going?'

'It's okay, only to an interview room.'

'Can't we do it here?'

'Sorry, these things have to be formally taped, for your own protection - and ours.'

'Right, new to me all this malarkey,' he said as he was led the short walk to interview room three.

'Take a seat, Mr Armstrong,' Marlowe told him.

'Paul, you can call me Paul.'

187

'Thanks,' Marlowe replied, 'you can call me Mr Marlowe.' No smile. He took two tape cassettes from his pocket, ripped off the cellophane and placed them in the machine.

'For the benefit of the tape would you please state your name?'

'Paul Armstrong.'

'Conducting this interview is DCI Marlowe and DC Lawson. Mr Armstrong, at this point in our enquiries you are not under arrest, merely helping with our enquiries. Are you happy to proceed?'

Armstrong nodded.

'Again, for the benefit of the tape...'

'Yes, I'm happy.'

'Thanks. Then we'll begin. Mr Armstrong - Paul,' he visibly relaxed when Jonno called him by his Christian name.

Marlowe sat back in his chair, arms crossed over his chest. Looked to Jonno and back to Armstrong. Jonno took the lead.

'Paul, you knew Michael Harrison I believe?'

'Oh yeah, since he was a little-un.'

'Friends then.'

'Yeah, good friends.'

'How do you feel about the fact he's dead, maybe even suffered a violent death?'

'Angry, bloody angry. That lad was like a son to me,' he said with sincerity.

'How about his friend, Robert Bacuss - you know him?'

'Can't say I do, why?' he replied, all the time keeping a deadpan face.

'All in good time. Let's talk about the *Blacksmiths Arms*. You still own the place?'

'Unfortunately, yes, sooner I get a buyer the bloody better.'

'And you live in the flat above the pub?'

'Y-e-a-h, you know I do.'

'You're partial to a game of poker they tell me?'

'Poker? Not me, I'm the world's worst player, can't keep a straight face.'

'Funny that, your partner, Mr Marriot tells us you're a bit of a player?'

He shook his head in denial. Jonno looked towards the DCI and raised his eyebrows - just a little - enough to let the boss know.

'When was the last time you pulled a pint?'

'In Blackie's?'

'Where else?'

'Oh, it's just that now and again, I help out in the *Swan* on Beverley Road, just when they need an extra pair of hands. In my place, not since we locked the door, months ago.'

'So the Blacksmiths's Arms hasn't opened its doors recently?'

'Would if the brewery would supply me, no chance of that happening with the amount of dosh I owe the brewery.'

'Then can you explain the yard full of empties?'

Armstrong shrugged his shoulders.

'Okay, we'll come back to that in a minute. Now, you own the scrap yard and the adjacent buildings?' The question Armstrong had been waiting for.

'I do indeed.' He sounded confident.

'Is Mr Marriot a partner?'

'In the business, not the actual properties, can I ask where this is leading to?'

They ignored the question.

The DCI leaned forward, elbows resting on the table.

'So, the motorcycle workshop, you confirm that you own the building?'

'Yep, it came as part and parcel with the yard.'

He was holding it together well thought the DCI, time to shake him up, he slid his folder across the desk in front of Jonno.

Jonno took over the questioning. 'You know we searched the yard?'

'And found bugger all,' Armstrong replied confidently.

'Also officers carried out a search of the lockup, your lockup Mr Armstrong.' First names disposed with.

'And you found nothing.' He sat back in his chair with his arms folded across his chest.

'I wouldn't quite say that. Our forensic teams also did a sweep of the room - know what they came up with?'

His facial expression changed from one of arrogance to one that wasn't quite sure what was coming next.

'Bleach.' Armstrong smiled, he could cope with that. 'And blood, Mr Armstrong - a large amount of blood. Can you explain that Mr Armstrong?'

'Cut myself a while back when I was shifting junk.'

The confidence was reappearing.

'That won't wash, sorry for the quip, according to the scientists the blood was fresh, no more than two or three days old at the most and I'm guessing it won't be yours.'

'Clever people the Crime Scene Examiners,' Jonno told him, 'they're the sort of people who *can* find a needle in a haystack.'

For all the tough guy appearance Armstrong was looking more than a little worried.

Marlowe had so far been keeping calm, but things were about to change. He sat forward in his chair and slammed the palms of both hands down, Armstrong visibly jumped in his chair.

'So where the hell have you taken, Robert Bacuss... Is he dead? Murdered? Just like you killed Michael Harrison?'

'I've told you I don't know anything, I've not killed anyone. How many more times do I have to tell you?' he rocked back in his chair, running his hands through his hair.

'One more time. WHERE IS ROBERT BACUSS?'

'No comment.'

'Funny,' said Marlowe, 'thought you might say that.'

'I'm not saying anything else until I've had a word with my solicitor.'

'You have a legal representative?'

He nodded. 'I'd like to make a call please.'

'Certainly, interview suspended.'

Jonno leaned across and stopped the tape recorder.

'What happens next,' asked Armstrong.

'My colleague,' he inclined his head towards Jonno. 'Detective Constable Lawson is going to arrest you for the murder of Michael Harrison and the kidnapping of Robert Arthur Bacuss.'

Armstrong was stunned into silence, the whole situation was way beyond his comprehension.

'We'll resume the interview in due course when your solicitor arrives. In the meantime, you will be taken back to the cells to wait.'

Marriot wasn't a stranger to police cells - he thought those days were over. He had never got used to the sound of the heavy door being slammed shut, the time he had actually spent inside as a guest of her Majesty had been the worst time of his life. Fair enough, he had known how to take care of himself and was left alone - but once that door was slammed shut... Sitting there on the bunk, leaning back against the wall he cursed Mick Harrison. He had convinced himself that if it hadn't been for the little shit, with his delusions of grandeur he wouldn't be sitting in a cell now.

He knew one thing for certain, he was *not* going to do time for something that had been an accident, if anyone *was* going to do time it wouldn't be him. He was certain he'd made the evidence point away from himself. So what if Paul got sent down? After all it was no skin off his nose, the scrap yard never made that much money anyway. On the other hand, with Armstrong out of the way he could do things, bring the place up to its full potential.

Young Bacuss was out of the way - so his cousin had gone and got himself run over by a ten-ton truck, there was no way they couldn't pin the twenty grand he had in his pouch on him. Okay, he'd lost a few quid, but as long as he could keep out of jail he saw himself as a winner.

Once the DNA results came back fingering Armstrong, he would be home free. There was just one thing he had to do, add a little fuel to the fire when he had the meeting with his brief.

Chapter 26

DI Gowan was sitting at his desk discussing the latest crime statistics with DS Jenny Bright when they were interrupted. 'Sir, Sarge, you got a minute?' Tanya stood in front of DI Gowan's desk.

'Are we finished, Jenny?'

'Yeah, we can't do anymore 'till I've had a word with the PI, see you in a bit. You okay, Tanya?'

'Yes, thanks, Sarge.'

'In that case, yes, what can we do for you, Tanya?' Gowan asked as he pushed back in his wheeled chair.

'Delicate, it's about the other business,' she brushed a stray hair away from her face and sounded a little uneasy. 'Can we go somewhere a little less public.'

'We'll take a break in the canteen.' He stood up and grabbed his jacket off the back of his chair.

'What are you having?' Gowan asked as they stood in the canteen queue.'

'Skinny latte, please,' Gowan shook his head. Skinny latte, mocha choca, Americano, why couldn't people just have plain ordinary coffee?

Sitting at a table with a view over the neighbouring houses along Gordon Street, Tanya relaxed - a little. She may have been partnered up with Gowan on the task, but he was still her boss.

'What's troubling you?' Gowan asked as he settled in his seat.

'Jokingly, I told the DCI, all the evidence points towards Sergeant Cleeves being responsible for nicking the drugs.'

Gowan smiled at the notion. 'He did mention it.'

'Yeah, well, here's the thing - I don't really know how to say it...'

'Do what I do, just spit it out, Tan.'

'Well, after the "joke" I went back through Sean Keane's file and the "joke" isn't funny anymore.'

'Explain and it better be good,' Gowan replied with all seriousness.

'As we know, Keane never had a criminal record, he always managed to worm his way out of things with a caution.'

'Yeah, thanks to his Uncle's expensive brief.'

'Anyway, I was... oh bugger it, did you know Sergeant Cleeves's lad is a junkie?' she blurted out.

'I know he had some problems in the past - what are you getting at, Tanya?'

'I did some follow ups with my informants about Keane, one of them, a horrible little man called Arty Major reckons Keane had recently started bragging about having a copper in his pocket.'

'What makes you to think he was talking about Trevor?'

'Well, if we go back a bit, the day the drugs went missing only Sergeant Cleeves had access to the evidence locker.'

'True, but as we know any copper in the station could have gone in there, nobody would think anything about it - it could be anyone at the nick.'

'Sir, the computer record of the drugs never been entered on the system has been deleted, the written log booking them in was signed by PC Roberts.'

'So what?' it doesn't prove Trevor was the one responsible.

'Robbo, PC Roberts was on long term sick leave at the time. He couldn't have booked it in.'

'Okay, you're on to something, but Trevor? Before we - you, start pointing the finger you have to have something concrete.' Tanya sat back dejected, her skinny latte going cold. 'Come on, back to work,' Gowan stood up. 'Let's not have any more conspiracy theories, okay? Sergeant Cleeves has been on the force a bloody long time and don't forget he's a pal of the boss. There's no way we want him to hear about any of this, or we'll both probably be transferred.'

Tanya followed the DI back to the squad room, keeping her mouth shut. She knew Cleeves and the DCI, they went back a long way. All it would need was for the DI to have a quiet word, sound him out. She was disappointed, she was on to something - and she'd prove it. She went back to her desk and rummaged through her bag for her personal address book. Found the number she wanted and dialled. 'Arty, its DC Etherington, I want another meet...'

'Oh c'mon, DC Etherington, you know I can't tell you anything.' Arty Major wiped his bulbous blue veined nose with the back of his hand then wiped it down his jeans. Disgusting.

'Arty, who's going to know? Sean Keane's dead, he can't touch you.'

'Yeah, but I'm no grass and he still has mates.' He said as he wiped his nose with the back of his hand then furtively looked over his shoulder, the last thing he needed in his miserable life was to be seen talking to a copper.

Tanya couldn't help but laugh out loud. 'What are you talking about, that's exactly what you are a paid confidential informant - a grass.'

'Yeah, but...'

'Never mind all the yeah buts, are you going to tell me or what?'

Major looked down on her. Six feet two inches tall, he dwarfed the detective who stood at five feet five inches tall, and that was when she was wearing heeled shoes. In the old days of height restrictions, Tanya wouldn't have even had a chance of joining the police force. By rights she should have been scared to talk to someone like Major, a scruffy looking, mean alcoholic who would do anything for his next drink. He had been known to break a head or two for cash when he was desperate enough. But with Tanya he was a pussy cat, they had an understanding - she was always good for a few quid when he could come up with a good tip off.

'Look,' she said staring up at him. 'All I want is the name of the pub that Keane and his so-called tame copper were seen drinking in, no more no less,' she took her bag off her shoulder and opened it. All of a sudden Major's facial expressions changed. 'You didn't think I wanted the info for nothing did you?'

Major shook his head vigorously, and hopped from one foot to the other, it looked like he was going to get pissed after all.

'You didn't get this from me, right?'

'Have I ever let you down? Just between us, no one will be any the wiser,' she lied. Of course she would do her best to keep it confidential, but, if push came to shove she would disclose where the information came from.

'It was in the Carlton.'

'When?'

'Oh for Christ's sake, how the hell do I know when it was, ages. I've had a couple of drinks since then!'

'Come on, Arty, think, it's important.'

'All I can say is, it must have been a Thursday, 'cos that's the day my benefits get paid into bank.'

'See, that wasn't too hard was it?' Tanya handed over a twenty pound note. 'Do me a favour, don't just piss it up the wall, go buy something to eat will you?' She said as she hung the bag over her shoulder.

Arty slipped the note into the pocket of his jeans. 'I will, as soon as I've had a drink.'

'Yeah, right, take care,' she replied and walked away knowing very well the twenty pound would be spent on booze before she even reached the Carlton.

She had heard of the Carlton but had never visited the club before and had a hell of a job finding the place. The private members club turned out to be above a block of shops along Hessle Road, only a ten minute walk away from the nick.

198

The entrance to the club was a single doorway sandwiched between a hairdressing salon and a betting shop. Tanya tread the lino worn stairs and pushed open the door. The place may have been a private members club, when she opened the door, she was surprised, the place was the pits. She could only guess at what kind of people were patrons of the place.

'You a member, luv?' The bar man asked as she walked across the scarred floor.

'Sort of,' she said, holding her warrant card for him to see.

'So I see, what can I do for you, officer?' he asked, placing his hands palm down on the polished bar top.

'Sean Keane, remember him?'

'Aye, knew him well, he was a member here until you lot shot his flippin head off.'

This was as far from the truth as you could get. Keane had taken it upon himself to walk into a hail of bullets during an armed siege. A siege where her close friend and colleague, DC Lee Kristianson had been held hostage and almost died.

'What about this bloke? She took out her mobile and held it for him to see, it showed a head shot of Sergeant Trevor Cleeves.

He looked closely and shook his head. 'Maybe, maybe not. Get a lot of people in here can't remember them all.'

'Do you keep your CCTV footage?'

He laughed out loud and splayed his arms. 'Does this look like the kind of place where we need CCTV? You having a drink?'

'Another time maybe, thanks for your time,' she said all the while thinking, thanks for nothing dickhead.

At the bottom of the stairs a thought occurred to her, the most likely place to have CCTV in the area would have to be the bookies next door. Above the exterior door was an omnidirectional dome camera. Oh yes, she thought, maybe her luck was changing. Outside the betting shop, the cigarette ends lay thick on the floor, it felt as if she was walking on a carpet. As the door opened, her eardrums were assaulted from the commentary blaring out of a large screen television. Punters stood newspapers in hand, yelling at the television screens.

Un-intimidated she elbowed her way through the punters. 'Is the manager available?' She almost had to shout through a glass divider partition, to a middle aged woman with badly applied make-up and bleached blonde hair. The fingers of her wrinkled hands were covered in rings.

'Alec, there's a copper here to see you,' she yelled above the noise from the speakers.' Tanya didn't think she looked so obvious. 'He's coming, luv, won't be a minute.'

Tanya saw a barrel shaped man with an almost comb-over hairstyle, come out of the private office. 'You looking for me, officer?' he dwarfed Tanya in height and width.

She held her up her warrant card. 'Detective Constable Etherington. You are?'

'Alec, Big Alec, the man of your dreams darlin'.' He did his best to do the James Bond accent but failed miserably. Tanya smiled, she'd had worse greetings, usually ending "...ard". 'I take it you're the manager?'

'I am, indeed, Big Alec here to help in *any way* I can,' he eyed her up and down suggestively.

'You can stop being so bloody offensive for a start or you can come down to the nick and answer my questions.'

'Sorry, officer, it's a habit, the women we usually get in here are - what shall I say - open to all manner of suggestion. Sorry about all that, yes, I'm the manager, Alec Stevens, how can I help?'

'Can we go somewhere a bit more private - and don't start again with the quips.'

Alec smiled. 'Yep, the office is this way,' he led her into the private office and gestured to a chair.

'I'm fine standing thanks,' she didn't want him perving at her legs. 'How long do you hang on to your CCTV footage?'

'Three months, have to for insurance purposes. What are you after, one of my customers up to no good?' His chair creaked under the strain.

'Not that I'm aware of. What sort of area does the exterior door camera cover?'

'It's bloody good, across the road, right from the doorway up to around fifty metres either direction.'

'So you get a picture of everyone entering and leaving the Carlton?'

'Aye, I suppose so, but confidentiality and all that we never check it unless we have a problem.'

'So, if I give you a date and time you'd be able to run me off a copy?'

'That I would.'

'How long will it take?'

'It's all stored on the computer hard-drive, so I reckon this time tomorrow?'

'That's great,' Tanya gave him the dates she thought most likely. 'See you tomorrow then,' she shook Big Alec's hand and left. Once on the street, she took out a miniature bottle of antibacterial gel from her bag and cleaned her hands.

All in all she was feeling quite pleased with herself, not that she disliked Sergeant Cleeves or held a grudge against him. But she needed to know, if he was responsible for stealing the drugs from the safe in the evidence locker, he could also be a conspirator in the kidnapping of Lee. She needed to know one way or the other.

If, and she thought it a big if, should Cleeves be seen with Keane on the CCTV, she was well on the way to proving her theory.

Chapter 27

The DCI was sat behind his desk going through the interview transcripts, when the phone rang breaking his concentration.

'Marlowe,' he recognised the voice, it was Sergeant Cleeves. 'Yes, Trevor, what can I do for you?'

'Marriot's brief arrived ten minutes ago and they want a word.'

'Sounds promising, thanks.'

His mood lifted a little. Was this a glimmer of hope? He was certainly hoping so. If they didn't get a break soon the Super would be banging on his door baying for his blood and his job.

Marlowe took off his reading glasses, dropped them to the desk and tried to rub away the gritty feeling in his eyes with his knuckles. Sighing, he pushed back in his chair, stood up and went through to the squad room looking around.

'Anyone seen, Jonno?

'Sorry, boss, not for a while.' DS Jenny Bright said as she looked up from her paperwork.

'The DI?'

Jenny shrugged her shoulders.

'Okay, Jenny, that means you're with me.'

'Where're we going?' she asked as she reached for her shoulder bag.

'You won't need that, we're only going to the interview room,' he smiled, 'apparently, Eddie Marriot has been having a word with his brief and we've been summoned.'

'Interesting,' she picked up a writing pad and pen.

'Yep, that's what I thought – let's go find out shall we?' he said thoughtfully. 'Ready?'

The DCI opened the door to interview room number three, the smell hit him immediately, he slyly glanced at Jenny who wrinkled her nose.

'DCI Marlowe, I must protest at my client being interviewed in such... such a disgustingly foul smelling room. I suggest we retire to another room right now.' Marriot's brief was fuming. He and Marriot had been sitting amongst the stench waiting for the past fifteen minutes. Marriot with a broad grin on his face, as his brief ranted.

This is going to be good thought the DCI, a smug villain and an arrogant brief.

'Good afternoon, you are?' Marlowe asked the studious young man sat next to Marriot. 'Peter Ireland, Mr Marriot's legal representative.' He definitely looked the part, expensive looking three piece suit, modern heavy rimmed spectacles and expertly waxed designer hair.

'I'd never have guessed,' the DCI mumbled to himself.

'Sorry I didn't quite catch that?'

'I said it smells in here.' Marlowe lied as he pulled out a chair and sat down. Jenny sat next to him and opened her A4 notebook and spread it on the table.

'Quite. Exactly, can we please move to a... a less offensive interview room?'

'Sorry, no can do, the other rooms are out of commission, this is the only space available. So, shall we get on with it?' He replied as he spread his file on the desk.

'My client would like to make a statement,' he sideways glanced towards Marriot - he nodded.

'So Mr Marriot, what would you like to tell us?'

'It's about that other lad, that pal of Mick's, whatcha call him, Bacuss?'

'Robert Bacuss, go on.'

Peter Ireland cut him short. 'DCI Marlowe, before we go any further my client would like to... er, make a deal,' he said nervously.

'How long have you been doing this job, Mr Ireland?'

Ireland hesitated before speaking. 'I have only recently qualified, this is my second case...'

'That explains it - I don't do deals, which you would have known should you have had a word with any of your colleagues that know me. So I say again, no deals. Now, gentlemen can we get on?' Jenny was loving it, keeping a straight face was a real struggle as Marriot's brief sat dumbstruck.

Marriot looked to his brief for guidance - nothing came, he just kept his head down.

'We're waiting,' Jenny said, looking up from her notes. Marlowe smiled. 'Robert Bacuss, you were saying?'

'Well, as I said before, I don't know him, but I know of him.'

'Explain...'

Was he jumping straight into the frying pan? His mind was a whirl. Then he thought fuck it. 'What do you want to know?'

'Everything. Start with what you know about the disappearance of, Robert Bacuss.'

He once more looked to his brief, this time he acknowledged with a nod. 'It was nothing to do with me, it was Harrison, he reckoned his mate needed teaching a lesson.'

'Teaching a lesson, how?'

'He was always ripping off the other students at the Uni, the ones who couldn't really afford to play poker, never mind lose their grant money. The idea was to fleece him at cards, you know. Let him win a few hands and then take him to the cleaners, leave him skint.'

'This card game did it take place in the *Blacksmiths's Arms?*'

'Yeah, that's right. Paul...'

'Paul Armstrong?'

He nodded. 'Paul opened up, got the place cleaned, took the for-sale sign down. He borrowed some booze from a pal and it was business as usual, well, for a couple of days at least.'

'What happened next?' Jenny asked.

'Well, he lost didn't he?'

'So why not just get what he owed from his father?'

'That was the original idea, get his old man to pay what he lost, but there was a change of plan. I had nowt to do with it. It was Mick and Paul, they reckoned we could get more than the seven grand he lost if we told his old man he'd been kidnapped.'

Marlowe let Jenny carry on with the questions while he studied Marriot.

'You went along with this?'

'No, not me, I was all for squeezing a few quid out of him, but kidnap? For God's sake there was no way I wanted to get involved with out like that. Told em straight, keep me out of it. Bloody hell, I reckon you'd get sent down for a long time for something like that?' He looked from Jenny to Marlowe and back again.

'So you don't know whether they went through with the actual kidnap?'

'Afraid not, made meself scarce as soon as they talked about it. Don't know if they went through with it or not.'

'Strange that, you not knowing anything about it, working so close to Mr Armstrong, then, low and behold your cousin Gordon gets knocked off his bike into the path of a ten ton truck and twenty thousand pounds get scattered all across the road. Now that *is* strange don't you think?'

'How much? Twenty grand, bloody hell, what was he doing with all that cash?'

'Delivering ransom money?

'I tell you, if he was it's a new one on me. Twenty grand! I can hardly believe it. He must have had some sort of deal going with Paul.'

'Paul Armstrong and your cousin, they mates then?'

'Not mates exactly, we've all had a drink together on occasions, that's about it, not mates.'

Yeah, yeah, Jenny thought to herself, as if.

The DCI sat back in his chair and folded his arms across his chest. 'So let me get this straight, you're telling me you were involved in the scam to fleece Robert Bacuss, but you deny having played any part in his abduction - correct?'

'That's about it, I don't know if they even went through with it. So yeah, that's it.'

'If, Armstrong were to abduct anyone where do you think he'd lock them up?'

'Only one place I can think of is the old band room, back of the motorbike workshop. Can't say as I can think of anywhere else.'

'We'll leave it there for now. What else can you tell us about Michael Harrison?'

'What about him, I've already told you he was a friend of Paul's.'

'So you have, we're more interested in the circumstances surrounding his death.'

Marriot sat there shaking his head. 'Don't know anything, didn't know he was dead 'till your colleague told me.'

'Whoever did kill him, why do you think they took him home and laid him on the bed?'

'Did they? Bloody strange. Maybe he wasn't dead and went home himself? You know died later?'

'Hmm, I was thinking along those lines myself,' the DCI said. 'Okay, Mr Marriot I think we'll leave it at that until we carry out further investigations into both cases. Thank you gentlemen.'

Jenny reached across the table and retrieved the twin tapes from the machine, initialled each in turn and handed one to Marriot's brief.

'You're free to leave, Mr Marriot, thanks for your cooperation. We will have to speak with you further, regarding the kidnapping of Robert Baccus.'

'Anything I can do to help.'

Marriot and his brief shook hands with both officers, he couldn't wait to get out of the place - he had a flight to book.

In the corridor they watched Marriot and his lawyer escorted through to the reception area. 'I'm not so sure about him at all, boss,' Jenny said as they walked back through to the CID squad room.

'I agree, there's a hell of a lot he reckons he doesn't know about his partner.'

'And he was bloody quick to come up with an answer to where the lad could be stashed.'

'Wondered if you'd pick up on that, he was way too bloody quick, didn't have to give it any thought whatsoever. Chase up the crime scene report on the lockup, see if Karina's found anything that can tie in Armstrong for when we next interview him.'

Chapter 28

Tanya had the foresight to have a with word the support officer manning the desk, should someone answering to Big Alec's description ask for her, she was definitely unavailable. She was itching to scrutinise the surveillance the lecherous bookmaker had left for her at the station reception. Her home was a one-bed roomed flat on the corner of Park Avenue and Princes Avenue. The rent was higher than she had originally wanted to pay, but the flat afforded a view directly across into the Pearson Park. Sitting crossed legged on the floor in front of her entertainment system, she reached across, put the DVD into the machine and pressed play. She was surprised at the quality of the playback, it was good - crisp and clear. There was near enough a full twenty four hours to fast forward, she watched patiently as the screen wound its way forward. The uniform branch at the Braemar Street nick worked a twelve hour shift, when the screen clock showed 6pm she pressed pause. Stood up and went through to the kitchen, returned a few minutes later with a cup of herbal tea, resuming her position on the floor she continued watching. She slowly forwarded the image, the screen clock showed 6.10pm.

'Yes,' she said out aloud as Sean Keane entered the doorway leading to the Carlton Club. 'C'mon,' she said to the television. Sure enough ten minutes later Sergeant

Trevor Cleeves, wearing civvies, followed Keane into the club. Tanya was now convinced she was on to something as she continued to watch, fast forwarding. An hour later Keane and Cleeves left the club together. At the foot of the stairs, she watched as the bobby passed over what looked like some sort of bundle, wrapped in a carrier bag, an exchange taking place. Keane reached into his inside pocket and retrieved a hefty looking envelope and passed it to Cleeves. The Sergeant and the villain shook hands and went their separate ways.

In the old days it was common practise for coppers and villains to use the same pubs and clubs - but these days it was highly unorthodox. What she had just watched without a doubt confirmed her suspicions. There was no way now that DI Gowan could say she was on some kind of "witch hunt".

Tanya took the folder containing her "research" and spread the pages on the floor, for the umpteenth time she reread the evidence. It was all there, what more evidence would she needed to convince the DI? She thought that maybe, Jenny, DS Bright might see things a little differently.

Tanya checked the time, it was still early, she picked up her mobile and keyed in DS Bright's number. 'Jenny - Sarge,' she said into her mobile.

'We're off duty, Jenny will do, this work or a social call?' she said reasonably light hearted down the telephone.

'Sorry to say, but it's a work issue,' she said, 'is there any chance of having a word?'

'Tonight?'

'I'd rather discuss it away from the station. I've turned something up that I really don't like the look of regarding the missing drugs.'

'The pub then, how about in the *Master's Bar* - half an hour?'

'Great, Sar... Jenny, see you in a bit.'

Tanya didn't like going behind the DI's back, but she really did need advice on what to do next without hanging herself out to dry.

Tanya gathered up the papers strewn across the floor, put them in an envelope along with the DVD and put them in her shoulder bag. After parking her Fiat 500 in the Bond Street car park, Tanya walked the short distance through the city centre streets to the Master's Bar. It was student night with half price cocktails and the place was reasonably full for a weekday evening. She stood just inside the entrance foyer and searched for Jenny. She spotted her towards the rear of the bar, Jenny waved as she saw Tanya shoulder her way through the students. A white wine spritzer was already waiting for her.

'Thanks, I'm ready for one of these,' she said as she sat in the quiet booth opposite Jenny.

Jenny let her settle herself, her junior colleague definitely looked worried about something. 'So what's so important that you've dragged me away from Coronation Street?'

'It's really awkward,' she picked up her spritzer, sipped and place the glass back down. 'As you know amongst other things I've been looking into the missing drugs in the

Keane fiasco,' she hesitated and drew a breath, 'as far as I can make out all the records have been tampered with.'

'Tampered with?' she picked up her own glass.

'Pages missing from the evidence locker log and things not entered on the computer when they should have.'

'Serious stuff, have you mentioned any of this to the boss or the DI?'

'Definitely not the boss and the DI thinks I'm reading things into the situation that aren't there. But I'm not - honest.' Another nervous sip and hesitation. 'I think it was Sergeant Cleeves.'

'I think you'd better tell me everything.'

The Detective Sergeant sat there listening to the story, throwing in the odd question along the way. 'And you have actually got a copy of the DVD of Cleeves and Keane together making some sort of exchange?'

'I have, it looks damning. Trevor, Sergeant Cleeves handing over something wrapped in a plastic carrier bag then accepting an envelope from Keane, putting it in his pocket then they shake hands and go their separate ways. Now you know why I didn't want to do this at the station.'

'Bloody hell, I'll get us some more drinks.' Jenny picked up her bag and went across to the bar. No wonder her junior didn't know what to do, Trevor was one of the boss's oldest friends and he wasn't going to like what he heard. 'This DVD, I need to see it before we take this any further,' she said when she returned with the drinks.

'Thought you might say that.' Tanya placed her bag on the table and took out the envelope containing her report and the DVD.

Jenny reached across the table, both her and Tanya holding the envelope. 'You realise there will be no turning back once I've seen this?' Tanya nodded and let go.

'You're sure you want me to take a look?'

'Sarge, I'm sure, when you have a look you'll see they weren't swapping Christmas cards.' Will you approach Trevor discreetly?'

'That depends on what I see, if it looks innocent, maybe, but if it's as you say we'll have to take it to the boss - together. Last chance Tan, have I to watch the DVD?' she asked, holding the unopened envelope in her hand.

'You have to, if as the DI says I'm reading too much into it, well, it could be my career over before it hardly started, but it has to be sorted one way or another.'

The decision had been made, the right one she hoped. At least the weight had been lifted from her shoulders if only temporarily. Tanya was convinced once Jenny had read through her file and watched the footage she would have to take her seriously.

An hour and a half later they headed their separate ways home. Jenny feeling apprehensive at what she would find in the file and on the DVD. Tanya was feeling a little better than she had an hour and a half ago - a trouble shared as they say. It may have been a trouble shared, but it didn't stop either of them from have a restless night. Jenny spent much of the evening reading and rereading the file well into the early hours. There was no way she could dispute the evidence that Tanya had gathered and the DVD - that was the icing on the cake.

Tanya's sleepless night resulted in her being in the office early. She was secretly dreading what might come. Jenny was already in the office by the time Tanya arrived. After first calling at the vending machine, Tanya placed a cup of coffee on the DS Bright's desk. 'Thanks,' she said as she looked up.

'Did you have a look at the DVD and the paperwork?'

'There's some pretty damning stuff, I don't think there's any other option than putting it all before the boss.'

'What about the DI? I don't want him thinking I've gone behind his back.'

'Don't worry about Dave, the boss said I was the supervising officer. If he has any issues he can take them up with me, you only did as you were told.'

'So you haven't had a word with the DCI yet?' Tanya asked as she stood nursing her own drink, holding the string of her tea bag dipping it in and out of the liquid.

'Not yet, but there's no time like the present,' she looked up and smiled. 'I'll give him a ring and see if he's got a few minutes.' Jenny picked up the phone and dialled. 'Boss, you got a few minutes?

'Indeed I have, what can I do for you,' Marlowe said into the phone.

'I wondered if Tanya and me could come through and have a word?'

'No problem, when you're ready I am.'

'Thanks, sir.' Jenny opened her desk drawer and took out the envelope containing the report. 'No time like the present.' Jenny stood up from her desk, picked up the envelope and looked at Tanya who gave out a big sigh. She didn't like it but knew it had to be done at some point. 'You ready?' Jenny knocked once on Marlowes door, opened it and they entered.

'Jenny, Tanya, what can I do for you?'

'It's a bit of tricky one, boss, Tanya has come up with something regarding the missing drugs and I don't think you're going to like what you hear.'

'Am I not? Then you had better sit down and tell me what I'm not going to want to hear.'

Tanya and the DS sat side by side on the office sofa, Tanya's face paled. 'Tanya?' said Jenny.

'What it is, it's err - you asked me to look into who might have originally removed the drugs from the evidence store,' she was careful in her choice of words refraining from saying stole.

Marlowe sat back in his chair. 'I did indeed, and I take it you know who that someone was?' His face was set, he didn't display any emotion. 'Jenny, I take it you've already scrutinised this information?'

'Yes, boss, I have - very carefully.'

'Okay, Tanya, let's hear it.'

For the following twenty minutes without interruption Tanya carefully went through the gathered evidence, finishing by passing the damning DVD across the desk. Marlowe didn't interrupt once, nor did he give any indication of agreeing or not agreeing.

'That was, what shall I say - very informative.'

'Boss, I didn't want to say anything because I know how close you and Sergeant Cleeves are,' she said at double speed, 'but the evidence speaks for itself.'

'I appreciate what you're saying, but as this allegation concerns a serving officer, regardless of who he is, in the circumstances I'll need a little time to read through everything myself - several times before I commit to anything. Okay?'

'Yes, sir,' Jenny echoed the comment.

'So, if you two wouldn't mind leaving me alone and I've no need to say this goes no further than the three of us, right?' Again they agreed.

Tanya and Jenny stood up. 'Sorry, boss, and thanks,' said the DC apologetically. Marlowe waved a hand in dismissal.

'For God's sake!' they heard the boss shout behind the closed door once they left the office.

'Well, thought that went better than I expected,' Tanya said to her Sergeant.

'To be honest, so did I, didn't know how he would take it, obviously he wasn't what you could call chuffed, but he'll do the right thing. For now we - you just keep your head down and get on with the job. I can assure you we'll be the first to know when he's made a decision, which I think will be sooner rather than later.'

Marlowe's night was one of maudlin thoughts. His old friend and long time colleague had created a crock of shit that had placed him in an impossible situation. Sitting in the *Daisy's* saloon with an empty bottle of wine in front of him and a bottle of Scotch, two thirds full, the other third in his glass. Archie lay snoring away on the cushion next to him. He picked up the glass and sipped, then sipped again.

Sighing, he placed the glass on the table. Outside the weather was on the turn the *Daisy* rolled on her moorings, as the wind blew relentlessly down the Beck. Marlowe looked up as the heavy rain pounded on the saloon skylights. Next to the glass of whisky the folder DC Etherington had collated lay open. He rested his elbows on the table edge, flicked over a page of the report, frustrated he slammed the folder shut. What was the point of going through it again? he had already read the material over and over again and arrived at the same conclusion, he didn't like it, but it was the only conclusion he could arrive at.

He needed a smoke before bed and took Archie's lead down from the hook, immediately Archie woke sensing it was his "out" time. Standing on the Beckside wrapped in his wax jacket with his Hull City bobble hat gradually getting soggier, he failed miserably to keep his cigarette dry.

Archie mooched in the grass at the end of his flexi-lead oblivious to the conditions. Marlowe moved to stand beneath the bare branches of a Poplar tree for protection from the downpour, his thoughts drifted to Robert Bacuss. Where the hell had they moved him to? Was he still alive? And what the hell would he tell Shag Pile Charlie if the lad turned up dead?

Bollocks he thought. 'Archie, come on,' he yelled to the mutt with his nose buried in the long grass. A quick tug on the flexi-lead brought Archie close. 'Come on, pal, let's get below and dry off.' The pair stepped aboard the narrow boat and went below. Dried off and standing in the hatchway Marlowe had another smoke, his thoughts all over the place dreading his meeting with Sergeant Trevor Cleeves in the morning.

Rab had been overjoyed when he thought he was to be freed, but now - cold, wet and shivering, he sat uncomfortably, his hands behind his back as he rested against the chilly wet corrugated sheeting of the Anderson Shelter. The side of his face felt raw from scraping it along the metal to free the rotting sack from his face. His eyes gradually adjusted to the dark, he hadn't a clue where he was or where he had been incarcerated, he thought it was maybe a cellar or some kind of storeroom.

Outside the weather was worsening, water seeped through the earth covered sheet metal ceiling and ran down the inside metal sheets gradually pooling on the rotten timber flooring. There was no respite from the wet, Rab was chilled to the bone.

Chapter 29

Tanya and Jenny had been summoned to the DCIs office 'Right the pair of you make yourselves comfortable.' The spare office chair was piled high with folders, leaving only one option, to lower themselves onto the sofa without losing any dignity. Marlowe took the well worn envelope out of his desk drawer placing it down in front of him. 'Well,' he said as he took off his reading glasses and dropping them onto the desk. 'I've had a read of this and, like it or not the evidence indeed speaks for itself and it doesn't leave any room for manoeuvre.'

Marlowe picked up his mug of cold tea and sipped, then spat it back in the mug. 'You will appreciate that before I can really say one way or another, I have to confront Sergeant Cleeves and listen to his side of the story. Agreed?'

Tanya shifted uneasily. 'I wouldn't have expected anything else, boss.'

'But saying that I think the outcome will be inevitable and I'm seeing two possible options available to us. Whichever option we go with will be your choice. When making your decision what I want you to bear in mind is this, Sergeant Cleeves has a previously unblemished record in the force.

'That we are aware of,' as she spoke, Jenny wished she'd chosen her words more carefully. 'Sorry, boss, but it had to be said. The options they are?'

'Well, Tanya here can arrest Sergeant Cleeves and we know what that would mean, the loss of his pension along with a custodial sentence.'

Tanya felt sick, she looked to Jenny. She knew it was a possibility, but hearing the actual words threw her. 'And the other?' she asked.

'Option two, he retires immediately on the grounds of ill health, keeps his pension and his reputation intact, and the whole unfortunate incident stays between the three of us.' There was another silence, longer this time. 'I'm not expecting an immediate answer and I'm not looking for the easy option either. I want you to go away and give it some serious thought. In the meantime, I'll have a meeting with Sergeant Cleeves and give him the opportunity to explain what the hell went on.'

The two officers left Marlowe's office. Both lost in their own thoughts.

'Well, say something, Sarge.'

'What do you want me to say? Go ahead and arrest him, get him locked up for a couple of years or let's give him a big pat on the back and send him a retirement card? This is a bloody mess. We'll talk later.'

Tanya didn't blame her for blowing a fuse, she was right, it was a bloody mess. Did *she* want to be responsible for Sergeant Cleeves being sent to prison? There was only one decision she could make, and that was not to ruin Sergeant Cleeves's life completely.

The DCI had already made his decision before the meeting with his two female team members, a decision he didn't like making, but it was the only one he could justify making.

'You wanted to see me, Phil?' Cleeves said as he walked into Marlowe's office.

'Sit down, Trevor, we need to have a word.' Marlowe sat forward in his chair resting his elbows on the desk

'This sounds serious, am I in for a bollocking or something?' Trying to make light of the situation - whatever that was.

'I wish that's all it was, Trev, I really do. I need to ask you something.'

'I'm all ears.'

'How well did you know Seane Keane?'

'Where's this come from?'

'Just answer the bloody question.'

'I didn't, the only time I ever spoke to the bloke was when he came into the nick.'

'You sure about that?'

'Course I'm bloody sure. What's going on here, Phil?'

'Just bear with me, Trevor, you're telling me you never had any kind of relationship with Keane?'

'Never, the bloke was a scumbag, why on earth would I be having any sort of relationship with him?'

Marlowe could see the Sergeant's face visibly paling and breaking into a sweat. He hoped to Christ, he wasn't going to have another heart attack.

'What if I told you we had evidence?'

'I'd say bloody show me, that's what I'd bloody say.'

The DCI spun the computer monitor around to face the Sergeant, tapped a key on the keyboard and the DVD started to play. Cleeves watched, gobsmacked, he ran a finger around the inside of his shirt collar.

'This isn't what it looks like.'

'What *does* it look like, Trevor? To me it looks like you handing something to a man you said you've never met outside of the station and, oh yes, receiving something in return?' What was it, Trevor, money in exchange of a parcel of Heroin? How much did you get, Trevor, a grand, five, ten? Enough for a nice holiday?'

The Sergeant stood up, almost pushing over his chair. 'I don't have to sit here and take this shit, Phil, I thought we were pals?'

'We are pals. Sit down, Trevor, and tell me what's been going on.'

Cleeves dropped heavily back onto the chair. 'I... I can explain,' the Sergeant slouched forward onto the desk. 'It all goes back to our Jamie, you know the crowd he got in with, piss heads and junkies the lot of them.'

'That was in the past, he was clean wasn't he?'

'Aye, well, that's what we thought. He'd started using again - and who was his supplier? Seane fucking Keane.'

'Why didn't you tell Keane to piss off and get Jamie into rehab?'

'No places, Phil, and Keane said if I didn't help him, he'd make sure everyone knew he was using again. I couldn't risk it, it would have broken his mother's heart all over again.'

223

'And now?'

'He's gone, reckoned he was going to stay with a mate in Glasgow, that's two months ago, we haven't heard a word since. I'm in the shit aren't I?'

'As far as you can get, mate, can't get any deeper. I knew it must have been someone in the station who stole the drugs, there was no other explanation and I needed to know who.' Marlowe placed the folder containing all the evidence on the desk and placed the flat of his hand on it. 'You know the score, Trevor, I can't just pretend none of this has happened...'

'No, I appreciate you've got to do the right thing.'

'Let me finish, Trev, the only people besides myself who know what happened are Jenny and Tanya, she's the one who uncovered all this shit.'

'Yeah, she is a tenacious little bugger.'

'I'm sure with a little persuading they will agree with what I'm going to suggest. You are going to go home, write your resignation and take early retirement to take effect immediately. You keep all this low key, no farewell parties, nothing. I'm sure with your heart condition, there won't be any questions asked.'

The Sergeant was close to tears. He had always known there was a chance of the events coming to light and they had. 'I don't deserve this, Phil, I really don't.'

'We go back a long way, Trev, a bloody long way and I'm giving you an out. If you agree with what I'm proposing it won't go any further and I'll shred this lot,' he held up the file Tanya had gathered. 'You leave here now; go on sick leave until your retirement papers come through and don't come back to the station.'

'I... I don't know what to say.'

'Say nothing and just leave, Trevor, just fucking leave.' Those were the last words Marlowe said to the Sergeant, he spun around in his chair and stared at the wall until he heard the office door open and close again.

Chapter 30

There was a tap on the door, Marlowe looked up. 'Boss, we've got the DNA results and the lab tests back on Harrisons body.'

'Right then, as Clint would say "make my day",' he said as he sat back in his chair gesturing for DS Bright to sit.

'A bit corny, even for you, boss, if you don't mind me saying?' Jenny pulled her chair towards Marlowe's desk and set her folder out in front of her.

'Even you are entitled to an opinion, Detective Sergeant.'

'Right, the samples that were taken from underneath Harrison's finger nails and his clothing, all came back as a positive match - a match to Paul Armstrong.'

'I'll be honest with you, Jenny, I'm surprised, would have put my money on it being Marriot's.'

'Any particular reason,' she asked as she leaned forward on her elbows.

'Besides not liking the bloke, none that would stand up in court. Anything else?'

'The gash on the back of his head,' she checked her notes. Looks like he was more than likely pushed or fell onto a sharp piece of metal two or three inches long, rather than being hit over the head with it, it went in the base of the skull, upwards into the brain.

Combine it with the fact that the oil residue found on the back of Harrison's clothing is a perfect match to the samples taken from the scrap-yard it all looks pretty conclusive.'

'So it would seem, get, Trev... or whoever's in charge of custody to chase up Armstrong's brief.' The DCI would find it strange without his old friend and colleague running the Custody Office.

Marlowe contemplated going for a quick smoke in the car park, but never got the chance, Armstrong's solicitor arrived. He hoped things weren't going go pear shaped, it was Darren Taylor, he was as sharp as the suit he wore.

'Mr Taylor, it's been a while,' said Marlowe.

'It certainly has, Detective Chief Inspector,' Taylor replied, holding out his hand. Taylor and Marlowe had crossed swords on a number of occasions.

'I take it you've had a word with your client?'

'I have.'

'Shall we?' Marlowe gestured to the interview room, then opened the door. 'Sorry about the smell in here, we're having problems with the God knows what and the other rooms are having some maintenance work carried out.'

'Phew, I see what you mean. Let's make this as quick as possible shall we?'

'That, Mr Taylor, depends on your client.'

Armstrong was already sat waiting. The officer keeping an eye on him stood up, nodded and left the room as Marlowe and Jenny entered.

Jenny turned on the tape machine as everyone settled into their seats. 'Mr Armstrong, we are recommencing the interview that took place earlier. You are still under caution, do you understand?' Armstrong nodded his agreement. 'Please confirm for the tape.'

'Yes, I understand,' he replied nervously showing none of the bravado shown by Marriot.

Jenny went on to state the time and named those present. Taylor sat beside Armstrong with a pensive look. Jenny slid the folder containing the case notes along the table. Marlowe flicked through the pages and then sat back in his chair.

'Now, Mr Armstrong, think very carefully before answering, you're positive you can't throw any light on the death of Michael Harrison?'

'I've already told you, none at all.' He was confident there was no way he could be tied into Harrison's death. Only he and Eddie knew what happened and it was Eddie who had given him the fatal push.

'You are certain about this?'

'My client has already answered the question,' interjected Taylor.

'So he has, but I'd like to hear him confirm his answer.'

Armstrong looked to his brief who nodded his agreement. 'Absolutely, I was surprised as anyone - didn't know anything about it until your colleague came to the yard and told us - me and Eddie.'

'So can you explain why your DNA was found on the clothing of Michael Harrison?'

The question caught Armstrong off guard, hesitating before answering. Both Jenny and Marlowe noticed the faltering.

'I... I don't know. Maybe it was from the last time he came to the yard, how do I know?

'That would explain things.'

Armstrong was relieved, it didn't seem as if they were going to push him on the subject.

'As you say that *could* explain the traces we found on his clothing, but that wouldn't explain the DNA underneath his fingernails would it?' Silence.

Armstrong sat shaking his head. 'This is bollocks,' he said, turning to Taylor.

Marlowe continued. 'Or the traces of Harrison's blood on your jacket?'

Armstrong sat forward and leaned across the table threateningly. 'How many times do I have to say it, I haven't a clue what you're talking about?'

'I disagree. I think it more likely the exchange happened when you grabbed him. Maybe he made a grab for you when you hit him over the head?'

'Hang on now, what are you saying? You think I killed him?' he was panicking, shaking his head from side to side in disbelief. There was no way they could stitch him up for this.

'The evidence speaks for itself, Mr. Armstrong.' Marlowe gently closed the folder. 'As far as I'm concerned - case closed,' he placed his hands down on his folder.

'Well your evidence is wrong,' he slapped the palms of his hands on the table. 'I'm not saying another word.'

'As you wish, Mr Armstrong.'

'Are we done, Detective Chief Inspector?' asked Taylor as he placed his pen on the table.

'Almost, can you throw any light on the whereabouts of Robert Bacuss?'

'Who?'

'You might know him better as, Rab, surely you remember him? You conspired along with Harrison to kidnap him.' Once again Armstrong sat shaking his head. 'We found evidence, evidence that Robert Arthur Bacuss was locked away in the back room of your workshop. Blood, DNA, you name it we found it along with your DNA and fingerprints.' Armstrong had been cut to the quick, he was speechless. 'Paul Armstrong, you are being arrested for the suspected murder of Michael Harrison and the kidnapping of Robert Arthur Bacuss. You do not have to say anything. But it may harm your defence if you do not mention when questioned something which you later rely on in court. Anything you do say may be given in evidence.'

Marlowe sat back in his chair and folded his arms across his chest. Jenny closed her A4 notebook and was about to stand up.

'I need to talk to my brief.'

Taylor looked across the table. 'DCI Marlowe?'

'Interview suspended at 4.50pm,' he leaned across and turned off the recorder. 'I'll send some coffees in.' Marlowe and Jenny left the interview room.

'What do you reckon that's about?'

'Who knows, Jenny, I'm off for a fag, get someone to take the coffees in.'

230

It was pissing down outside, Marlowe made a dash for the Perspex shed in the designated smoking area. He took out his cigarettes and lit up, it was strange, he was used to being in the company of Sergeant Cleeves whenever he went for a smoke. He hadn't heard a word from his old friend since their controversial meeting in which he'd been given the option, resign or be arrested.

Eddie Marriot had also been busy. His case was packed, his wallet and passport lay on the coffee table with the laptop computer. The printer buzzed into action as it printed off his ticket to Tenerife, flying from Doncaster, Robin Hood Airport that evening

Out the corner of his eye Marlowe saw Jenny waving from the doorway trying to catch his attention. He dropped his cigarette to the floor and heard it hiss as it fell into a puddle. Collar up, he made another dash.

'Armstrong and his brief, they want to talk,' she said as he dashed through the open door.

'Did he give you a clue?' He asked as he turned down the collar of his jacket.

'Nope.'

'Then let's go and find out.'

Taking their seats once again in the interview room, Jenny turned on the tape machine. 'Interview recommenced at 5.10pm.'

'DCI Marlowe, my client would like to make a statement.'

'We're listening.'

Jenny opened her notebook.

'I've been stitched up - it was Eddie,' Armstrong blurted out.

'What was Eddie?'

'He was the one that did it.'

'You're talking in riddles, Mr Armstrong. I presume you are referring to your partner Eddie Marriot, what exactly has he done?'

'Mick, he... he was the one that killed him. Eddie reckoned it was an accident. They'd had an argument, see, he said he pushed Mick and he went down and banged his head - simple as that. He must have planted all the evidence against me. Well, I'm not going down for something I'VE NOT DONE.'

'If it was an accident, why didn't one of you call the police?'

'We couldn't could we - not with Bacuss in the lockup.'

'I take it you are confessing to the kidnapping of Robert Arthur Bacuss?' Armstrong nodded his head.

'For the benefit of the tape, please,' asked Jenny.

'Yes,' a short, curt reply.

Marlowe felt slightly light headed, he didn't know whether it was the nicotine hit or the shock of the confession.

'So what was, Gordon Evans, role in all of this?'

'No idea what you're talking about.'

'Eddie's cousin the postie, the one who got himself crushed under the front wheels of a truck, with twenty grand in his mail pouch.'

'You telling me he was delivering the ransom money? Cos it's a new one on me - things hadn't got that far. The double crossing bastard. Bastard.'

'So the lad?

'Which one?'

'Let's start with Harrison, it was you that took him back to his flat?

'Had to, the least I could do was give him a little dignity,' he said, glassy eyed.

'And Bacuss, is he still alive?'

'Course he bloody is, I told you I'm no killer.'

'Then where is he?' the room seemed exceptionally quiet as they waited for the reply.

'In the Anderson Shelter at the bottom of me mam's garden.'

Jenny pushed a piece of paper across the desk and gave Armstrong a pen. 'The address, write it down.'

Armstrong wrote down the details and pushed the paper back across the desk. 'Interview suspended,' he said as he read. Jenny turned off the tape. Both Marlowe and Jenny immediately stood up and left the room. 'Take him to the cells,' Jenny said to the uniformed officer waiting in the corridor.

As Armstrong was being led from the room Marlowe asked. 'Out of curiosity, what was the plan when this was all over?'

'Me, I was hoping to get me pub back.'

'Marriot?'

'Heading off to warmer climes.'

The rain beat down relentlessly, the earth pile high on the Anderson shelter was saturated, the constant drip had now turned into a steady stream, like a slow running tap. Rab lay on the rotting boards, his face raw and bleeding from how he had rubbed against the metal to free the rotting hood. He lay kicking out with his legs against the rotting timber door. Thud, thud, again and again, he kicked out with what strength he had left. Breathless, he rested briefly. His clothes soaked, he lay shivering, then started all over again. Lying on his back, he kicked out planting both feet against the rotting timber of the door, then it happened a board fell free. Relentlessly he kicked again and again, eventually freeing another board, creating a wider opening. 'Shit,' he said as the tape around his ankles snagged on a rusting screw. He tugged to free himself, pulling back the tape the frayed and snapped. After regaining his breath, he slithered legs first like a snake through the opening he found himself in a shallow stair well.

It was as dark outside as it was in the shelter. The fresh air was a welcome relief after the musty odour. He eased himself on the bottom step and edged his way backwards up the three steps. The torrential rain did little to lift his spirits - he was already soaked from head to toe and had hardly any strength left in his legs. Regardless of the weakness in his legs, he managed to get himself into the kneeling position. With the aid of a Bramble bush that scraped and scratched him until he bled, he managed to stand, leaning into the thorns he looked around, nothing just darkness he was totally disorientated. Rab lay back against the thorns that

234

cut into his flesh, he had had enough, he needed to rest before carrying on. With the support of the branches he managed to remain standing, like a bunch of rags he hung from the bush, then the inevitable happened, exhausted his eyes closed.

Marlowe relayed Armstrong's mother's address to the dispatcher controller. 'Anyone in the vicinity I want them there ASAP,' he said into his mobile as they walked into the squad room. 'Don't take any excuses, and I want NorthSea Ferries and all the local airports put on the lookout for Eddie Marriot.' A sense of energy flowed through the room. 'Dave, Jonno, you're with me and Jenny outside now.'

DI Dave Gowan grabbed his jacket. Jonno stumbled, knocking over a chair as they raced after Marlowe, who was already heading for the car-park. The road surface of the A63 Clive Sullivan Way was awash with rain water. Reaching speeds in excess of eighty miles per hour Marlowe's Mondeo was almost aquaplaning. Jenny, sat in the front passenger seat besides the DCI, her knuckles white as she gripped the sides of her seat all the while staring through the windscreen, the wipers slapping away in double time. In the rear seats Dave Gowan and Jonno didn't fair any better.

As they neared the North Ferriby turn off, blue flashing lights could be seen ahead of them. Still driving as though they were on the dual carriageway, the DCI had his foot hard down on the accelerator pedal. Marlowe's concentration wavered for a second they were almost upon the flashing blue lights of the traffic car. A uniformed officer wearing a high visibility vest stood at the back end of his vehicle waving a torch, the beam flashing from side to side to get Marlowe's attention. Foot off the accelerator and slammed onto the brake, the Mondeo skidded along the wet tarmac coming to a stop within a couple of feet of the stop light of the stationary patrol car.

The traffic officer approached the Mondeo. 'Bloody hell, sir, cut that a bit close didn't you?' he said as the DCI opened the car door.

'Didn't hit you, did I?' snapped Marlowe.

'No, but...'

'Then what's your problem? Where's your oppo?'

'Taking a look around, sir.'

Marlowe reached under the driving seat and pulled out a torch shining the beam into the officer's face. 'Right, lead the way.'

Apart from the traffic officer no one was wearing any wet gear. The rain continued to beat down, soaking them through as they followed. They saw the officer's colleague shouting and hammering on the front door of the bungalow in frustration. Inside Armstrong's arthritic mother was struggling to get out of her chair. 'Police, open the door.' He continued to hammer.

'Oi, leave it,' yelled Marlowe, 'get around the back.'

Following the beam of the torches the entourage made their way down the long overgrown drive. Marlowe stumbled over the ruts as he flashed the torch beam in all directions.

'There,' shouted the lead uniform, shining the beam of his torch to the left. The grass was knee high, they stumbled over the uneven ground towards a hillock - the Anderson shelter. The torch beams shone through the rain, and then they saw him. 'Call for an ambulance the officer yelled as he stumbled through the undergrowth. Rab hung like a scarecrow from the ragged thorns of the bramble bush. Bruised and battered, blood ran in rivulets' down his face.

The DCI shoved the uniform aside. The lad didn't look so good, with two hands, he took a hold of Rab's head. 'Rab, can you hear me?' No response. 'Rab, it's the police you're safe. Rab?' Marlowe leaned in close, he could feel the warm breath coming from his mouth. 'Get him down,' he told the uniforms.

As gently as they could, they lifted Rab free from the thorns that impaled his clothing and skin. Carefully they laid him on the wet grass. Jenny dropped down beside him. 'Give me your jacket,' she ordered the uniform. He stripped off the jacket as fast as he could. Jenny still kneeling in the grass and mud wrapped it around Rab. 'He's in a bad way,' she said, looking up to Marlowe.

'Chase up that ambulance.' Please don't let him die, he said in his head.

'ETA two minute's, boss, Jonno said shutting down his mobile. Jenny now almost lay atop of the lad trying to give him some body heat.

'I'll ring Sha... Bacuss, tell him to meet us at the Infirmary.'

The sound of the ambulances blues and twos could be heard approaching. Skilfully, the Paramedic reversed the vehicle down the rutted drive with urgency. Both doors flew open. The first medic grabbed his bag and ran to Rab's aid, while his partner pulled out the patient trolley from the rear.

Everyone stood aside while the Paramedics worked. 'Lucky lad,' the Medic told them, 'seems you got here just in time. Another half an hour and I don't think we'd be rushing,' he turned to Jenny. 'Well done.'

They watched as Rab was wrapped in blankets, strapped to the trolley, an oxygen mask placed over his face and then he was loaded into the back of the vehicle. It seemed to take an age for the medics to ensure he was stable. Once satisfied the doors shut, the blues and twos turned on and the emergency vehicle headed back to the Hull Royal Infirmary.

'Leave us a couple of torches,' Marlowe told the traffic cops before they returned to their vehicle.

'Get scene of crime down here,' Gowan told Jonno.

'Already on it,' he said, gesturing to his mobile.

Armed with their torches they aimed the beams into the shelter. 'For God's sake, how could they leave him in there?' Jenny asked as she scanned the interior, the floor was now around four inches deep with rain water, all the while more was pouring in. 'Not much hope for the CSEs.'

More vehicles arrived and a stream of lights headed down the rutted path toward them. Once Marlowe was sure the sodden crime scene had been secured the sopping officers climbed back into the Mondeo.

'I'll drop you back at the nick, then I'll go face the music with Shag Pile.'

'At least we got the lad back alive,' Dave Gowan replied as he ran his hands across his wet face.